MW00413151

SPEAK NO EVIL

RUSTIC KNOLL BIBLE CAMP SERIES, BOOK 2

MARY L. HAMILTON

SPEAK NO EVIL

Rustic Knoll Bible Camp Series Book 2

Mary L. Hamilton

©2014 by Mary L. Hamilton

All rights reserved. No portion of this book may be reproduced, stored in a retrieval system, or transmitted in any form or by any means— electronic, mechanical, photocopy, recording, scanning, or other— except for brief quotations in critical reviews or articles, without the prior written permission of the author.

Scriptures quoted by permission. Quotations designated (NIV) are from THE HOLY BIBLE:NEW INTERNATIONAL ®. NIV®. Copyright © 1973, 1978, 1984, 2011 by Biblica. All rights reserved worldwide.

Cover design by AMDesignStudios.net.

Camp map is ©Mary Hamilton.

This novel is a work of fiction. Names, characters, places, and incidents are either products of the author's imagination or used fictitiously. All characters are fictional, and any similarity to people living or dead is purely coincidental.

Second Edition March 2017

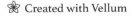 Created with Vellum

This book is dedicated to my late parents,
Rev. Paul and Florence Watson
and to
Lutherdale Bible Camp
where they served for nearly 20 years.
May the Lord continually bless Lutherdale's ministry.

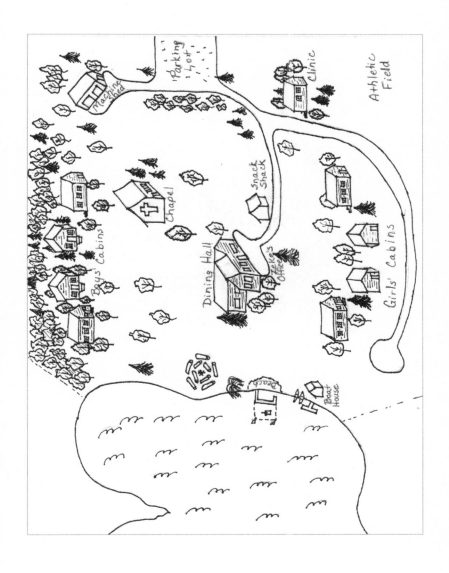

1

Taylor Dixon riveted his gaze to the red Corvette pulling into the parking lot of Rustic Knoll Bible Camp. Its supercharged engine purred like a monster cat as the 'Vette prowled the rows of parked cars hunting a space of its own, finally settling across two slots in the back row.

Forgetting Dad's command to unload the car, Taylor stuffed his auto magazine into his pillow and put some distance between himself and the family's van. He drank in the Corvette's sleek body, his heart racing with the engine as the driver revved it up before shutting off the machine. Oh, for a closer look, but he didn't dare. Not with Dad nearby. His younger sister came up and leaned into him.

"Nice." Marissa drew the word out, keeping her voice low.

"It's awesome."

Her finger poked his side. "I wasn't talking about the car."

Taylor glanced sideways at her, then looked back at the 'Vette.

A boy about Taylor's age emerged from the passenger's seat. The kid stretched and surveyed the parking lot, a smug grin hugging his face. His eyes met Taylor's. One eyebrow arched as he lifted his chin high. His grin changed to a smirk before his gaze slid over to Marissa.

Wait. Was that a wink?

Marissa stiffened, caught her breath and stifled a squeal. She squeezed Taylor's arm, her fingernails biting into the soft skin of his inner elbow. But before he had time to consider some guy flirting with his sister, Dad finger-thumped his head.

"Don't get any ideas. You're not getting your driver's license. I don't want you anywhere near a car like that until you're eighteen and I'm not responsible for you anymore."

Taylor huffed and turned back to their drab gray minivan. "Dad, I'm at camp, remember? Swimming? Softball? Sermons? No cars."

"Yeah, so quit drooling and get your stuff out of the car. I don't want to be here all day."

Ducking under the liftback, Taylor muttered while he pulled out his duffle and sleeping bag. "I wasn't drooling."

Reaching for her pillow, Marissa giggled and whispered, "I was."

Taylor growled. "Forget it, Riss. He's a stuck-up snob."

"How do you know? You haven't even met him." She didn't bother to keep her voice down.

"Didn't you see the way he looked down his nose at us? He thinks he's hot because he came to camp in a 'Vette."

"Oh, he's hot even without the car. Maybe he looked down his nose at you, but he winked at me. Admit it. You saw it, too." Marissa struggled to pull her suitcase out of the van. "Ugh! Can you get that out for me?"

Taylor tugged on her overstuffed bag. "What's in here? You must've packed your whole bedroom." He hauled it out and set it on the ground.

"Everybody ready?" Mom grabbed her purse and closed the passenger door.

Dad shut the liftback door. Even though it was summer, he

wore his football coach's shirt. Dad's hefty build and graying buzz-cut hair were so different from Taylor's, few kids at school ever guessed he was Coach Dixon's son. Before Taylor took two steps with his own duffle bag on wheels, Dad clamped a vise grip on his shoulder. "Take your sister's suitcase. It's too heavy for her."

Taylor handed Marissa his pillow and sleeping bag, then dragged both their suitcases across the gravel parking lot. Marissa's had to be loaded with bricks. He stopped to switch hands. "Riss, we're only here for a week. Why'd you bring so much stuff?"

"I only brought what I need." Marissa repositioned her purse strap on her shoulder, then shifted the pillows to her other arm. "Taybo, I can't wait until you have a car like that Corvette."

Dad grunted. "In his dreams."

"His dreams will come true. One day, he'll be a famous race car driver and he'll get to drive Mustangs and Corvettes and all kinds of hot cars." She threw a smile Taylor's way. "And he'll take his favorite sister for a ride in them, too. Won't you?"

Dad shot Taylor a warning look. "He'll stay miles away from those cars if he knows what's good for him."

Arguing was useless, but Taylor couldn't help it. "Can't I at least get my license? I'm almost sixteen. All my friends are learning to drive, and I pulled my grades up like you wanted."

"Prove to me you deserve to drive." Dad might as well have been talking to one of his players.

"How? What do I have to do?"

"Show me you're responsible by staying out of trouble."

Like that would ever happen. Not as long as he kept getting blamed for Marissa's adventures. Taylor gave up, but Marissa continued the argument.

"Daddy, just because Jesse stole a car and went to jail doesn't mean Taylor will, too."

"Princess, you can stick up for your brother all you want, but I know boys. Taylor hung around Jesse and those delinquent friends of his. Who knows what they taught him?"

Mom threw a glance at them over her shoulder. "Can we not talk about this right now?"

Taylor slowed, letting the others walk ahead of him. Marissa was only thirteen but the way things were going, she'd get her license before he did. The family princess. And Jesse was the prince, Dad's favorite from the moment he put on a football uniform.

Where does that leave me? Stuck between a princess and a prince.

Taylor yanked hard on Marissa's suitcase and joined the rest of his family at the end of the check-in line. Nurse Willie manned the registration table like last year, wearing her weird hat with the fishing lures all over it. He'd almost persuaded Mom to let him stay home this summer. But then Marissa decided camp sounded like fun, and if she was going, he had to go, too.

Taylor searched the line for a familiar face, but didn't recognize anyone from last year. Whenever they inched forward, Dad checked his watch and sighed loud enough for everyone nearby to hear.

Marissa nudged Taylor's arm. "Tell me what the buildings are so I don't get lost. That one must be the church." She pointed to the chapel with its steep roof and blue cross-shaped window.

Taylor nodded toward the nearest low building with redwood stained siding. "That's the dining hall. The girls' cabins are over on the other side of it. Guys cabins are over this way, past the chapel."

"What's that little hut over there?" Marissa indicated the small building at one end of the dining hall.

"That's the Snack Shack. A message board is posted on the outside wall on the other side. You'll need to look there for your Rec team assignment and daily activities."

"Will we be on the same rec team?"

"I hope not. You're such a klutz, we'd never win anything."

"Hey!" Marissa punched his arm and turned her back to him, acting insulted.

But it was true. Marissa was as uncoordinated as Jesse was athletic.

Jesse. Even though five years separated them, Jesse had always let him tag along, announcing to his friends, "Hey everybody! Taylor's here. Say hi to my little brother." Had there really been a note of pride in Jesse's voice or was it his imagination, wishful thinking on his part? For a while, he'd taken on his brother's shuffling walk and the way he pointed both thumbs in the air when something pleased him. But Jesse had often teased him, too, and they'd had their fights. Still, when Jesse was around to toss a football or shoot hoops, it was easier to handle the lack of attention from Dad. Hopefully prison wouldn't change his brother too much by the time he got out.

When they finally reached the check-in table set up in the shade of a large oak tree, Mom handed their health forms to Nurse Willie.

Marissa eyed Willie, her white hair a contrast with her dark skin, and the bucket hat adorned with fishing lures atop her head. "Cool hat."

Dad rolled his eyes and walked away, shaking his head.

"Thank you." Willie scanned their health forms. "You must be Taylor's sister. Good to see you again, Taylor. Looks like you've grown a couple inches since last year." She held the papers out so the counselor sitting next to her could see the names. "Lauren, this is Taylor Dixon and his sister, Marissa. Taylor was here last year."

"Hi! Welcome to Rustic Knoll." Lauren's smile showed off perfectly white teeth. A bit of red chewing gum peeked from the corner of her mouth. "Marissa and Taylor?" She snapped her gum and slid her finger down a list of names. After highlighting two in pink, she looked up. "Okay, Marissa, you are in Magnolia

Cabin. That's back ovet here." She pointed to the right behind her back. "And Taylor, you're in Spruce Cabin."

"I know where it is." Taylor let go of Marissa's suitcase and flexed his hand a few times. No way was he dragging that thing to the cabin for her. He glanced again down the check-in line for a familiar face. He knew the kid with red hair who was standing with the one wearing dark glasses.

Brady and Steven were in his cabin last year, but he didn't expect a friendly greeting from them. Not after all the trouble he gave them. The girl with short blonde hair talking with Brady and Steven was Claire Thompson. No surprise there. She and Steven and Brady were buddies. Would Claire remember him? Taylor caught her eye and waved, but she barely lifted a hand before turning away. Not the response he'd hoped for.

"Who's that? She's cute!" Marissa sounded incredulous, as if surprised he would know any pretty girls.

"Yeah, but she didn't look too impressed," Dad said. "I'd say she's a little out of your league." He prodded Taylor away from the check-in table. "Show me to your cabin, Hot Shot."

"Aren't you going to help Marissa with her suitcase?" Anything to keep Dad from accompanying him to the cabin.

Mom moved the suitcase away from the check-in table. "We girls can manage." She kissed Taylor's cheek, and gave him a quick hug. "Bye, honey. Have a good week. We'll see you on Saturday." Mom took hold of the suitcase handle. "C'mon, Marissa."

Dad urged Taylor forward. "Let's go."

Taylor yanked his bag behind him, using his chin-length brown hair to cover the frown on his face. Last year, Mom brought him to camp while Dad stayed home with Marissa. But with both him and Riss coming to camp this year, Mom talked Dad into joining them for a "family outing." At least with Marissa here, he wouldn't have to endure Mom making his bed and hanging up his clothes like last year. But he could only hope no one else was in the cabin to hear Dad's opinions.

They skirted the chapel, walking alongside the windows that looked out over the lake. Dad peered inside. "How often do they make you go to church here?"

"All morning, plus another worship session in the evening."

"Worship session? You mean like Sunday church?"

Taylor shrugged. "Kinda, but the music's more like our kind of music." His roller bag bounced and tipped when they reached the end of the sidewalk.

"You listen to what the preacher says?"

"Sometimes." Taylor righted the bag and tugged on it. The wheels didn't work so well in the grass.

"Sometimes? If you want your license, you'd better pay attention all the time, y'hear? Your mother and I don't need another jailbird, like your no-good brother." Dad whacked the back of Taylor's head. Not hard, but his wedding ring bit into Taylor's skull.

"Ow!" Taylor dropped his sleeping bag and rubbed his head. "I'm not Jesse. Okay?"

"We'll see. You listen to that preacher every time he talks. Do you understand?"

"Okay!" Taylor moved out of ring-shot range. Nothing he did would ever convince Dad he wasn't running in Jesse's footsteps. His brother, the star player on the school's football team, could do no wrong. But he'd fooled everyone, including Dad whose dreams of borrowed glory got smashed when Jesse quit the team, got arrested and sent to prison.

They skirted the giant blue spruce tree that identified the cabin and Taylor climbed the two concrete steps to the front door. The screen door squeaked as they entered and Taylor led the way through the common room, its worn couches and ragged armchairs perfect for teenage boys to lounge on.

Dad wasted no time finding fault. "Rustic Knoll, huh? Rusty nail is more like it. And we pay good money for this."

Taylor entered the bunkroom and tossed his sleeping bag onto the first empty bed, shoving his duffle bag underneath. A couple of sleeping bags lay tossed on other bunks, but the cabin was empty at the moment. Now, if he could get rid of Dad before anyone else arrived. He dug his hands into his pockets.

"This is it. Not much to it."

The screen door squeaked open and slammed shut. A young man with dark skin and close cut hair unlocked the door to the counselor's room before glancing in their direction. He strode toward them and extended his hand.

"Hi! I'm Harris Franks, your counselor. And you are?"

"Taylor Dixon." He shook the counselor's hand then watched as Harris shook Dad's hand. Dad liked to test the strength of guys' handshakes. Taylor didn't see the customary wince, but considering those biceps, he wasn't surprised. When did a counselor get time to work out?

Dad released Harris's hand. "You're here all summer? How much they pay you to live in this dump?"

Harris's brows popped up and an uncertain smile pulled at the corners of his mouth. His gaze flicked from Dad to Taylor and back to Dad. Taylor hung his head, his long bangs falling over his face.

Harris tapped his keys against his thigh. "I don't do it for the money."

"Uh-huh. You in college?" Dad eyed Harris who stood half a head taller but only half as wide. "Yes, sir."

"What's your major?"

"I'm in a Biblical Studies program, planning to enter the ministry."

"Gonna be a pastor?" Dad grunted. "Good for you. Maybe some of it'll rub off on Taylor this week. Keep your eye on him. He likes to get into trouble."

Taylor peeked at Harris through strands of brown hair.

"Don't worry, Mr. Dixon. I'm sure Taylor and I will get along fine." Harris stepped between them and gently guided Dad toward the door. "If we do have any problems, how do you suggest I discipline Taylor?"

"Well now, I'm not one for smackin' kids around..." Dad's voice trailed off as they exited the cabin.

Except for vise grips and brain thumps. But it was the verbal smack-downs that hurt the most.

"Taylor?" Dad called from the front steps. "You keep an eye on your sister this week."

"Yeah, I know." Having the Princess at camp with him was going to be a royal pain.

2

Taylor unrolled his sleeping bag, grabbed his pillow and heaved it to the end of the bed. Personal guard for the Princess, that's all he was. And without the athletic ability equaling Jesse's, he had no hope of Dad taking notice of him. It was fun living in Jesse's shadow when he took the team to State. But the occasional bits of glory dust that settled on him turned to ashes with Jesse's conviction. Now, Taylor might as well be covered in soot. Dad never spent time with him the way he did with Jesse. At least he didn't have to put up with the constant criticism Jesse had endured. But couldn't Dad notice him for something more than looking after Marissa? Couldn't they watch a car race together or something?

Taylor plopped down on his bed and stretched out, pulling the car magazine from inside his pillowcase. He'd go look for his buddy, Nick, in a minute, after he finished checking out the rest of these Mustangs and Camaros.

Other campers arrived and claimed bunks, including the kid from the Corvette. He was tall with a sturdy build and sand-colored hair that ended just above his ears. His shorts hung low on his hips, revealing boxers with Corvettes on them. Cute. The label on his shorts wasn't exactly a discount brand, either. The kid dumped his stuff on a bunk, then leaned across the empty one between them and introduced himself. "Luke Erickson." He cocked his head to read the title of Taylor's magazine and wrinkled his nose. "You like those?"

"Yeah. Something wrong with that?"

Luke shrugged and unrolled his bedding. "I guess not, if you like common cars. My dad's getting the new 'Vette, a custom job. I get his old one." He stood and faced Taylor. "I almost talked him into letting me drive it up here, told him I needed to get used to driving it." Luke laughed out loud. "That's like saying you have to get used to eating steak."

Taylor closed his magazine and laid it on the bed. The images inside had lost their appeal.

Luke looked around. "Hey, where's the toilet in this place?"

Taylor pointed in the direction of the bathroom. Familiar voices outside the cabin grew louder. *Brady and Steven? Surely, we're not all in the same cabin again this year.* The screen door squeaked and slammed. Brady led the way into the bunkroom, guiding Steven in his dark glasses and pulling a suitcase behind him. Brady stopped short when he saw Taylor.

Steven let go of Brady's arm and reached out, feeling for the bed in front of him, the empty one between Taylor and Corvette Boy. "Is this one taken?"

Brady glanced at the other bunks. "I don't think you want—"

Taylor interrupted. "Yeah, it's open. Take it. And Brady can have the top bunk."

Brady shook his head. "I'm in Ash Cabin this year."

"Taylor?" Steven's head turned in his direction.

"Yup. Cabin buddies again. Exciting, huh?"

Luke returned from the bathroom and stuck his hand out toward Steven and Brady. "Hi, I'm Luke."

Steven's head swiveled to the right. "Hey, I'm Steven. This is Brady." Brady reached around Steven to shake, but when Steven failed to acknowledge the gesture, Luke's fingers curled into his palm and he pulled his hand back.

Taylor suppressed a grin. He'd made a similar mistake last year, before he knew Steven was blind. How long before Luke figured it out?

Luke eyed Steven. A single chuckle escaped his lips. "What's with the shades? Are you, like, a celebrity or rock star or something?"

Steven moved forward to claim the bed between Taylor and Luke. "Yep, I'm traveling incognito. Don't tell anybody, okay?"

Brady dropped Steven's sleeping bag and pillow on the bed. His eyes cut to Taylor, a grin curling his lips.

Luke's gaze hopped between Steven, Brady and Taylor. "Okay, what's the joke?"

"What? You don't recognize Steven Miller?" Taylor rolled his eyes. "How could you not know him? Maybe you need to forget those fancy sports cars and pay more attention to the real world." He pushed himself off the bed and headed out the door, muttering loud enough for the others to hear. "Sheesh, he brags about his dad's 'Vette, but doesn't recognize Steven Miller when he sees him. What a loser!"

Taylor found Nick in Elm cabin and told him about the joke he'd played on Luke. "He's gotta be filthy rich if his dad can afford to give him a Corvette."

Nick rummaged through the clothes in his suitcase. "What's the matter with that? You jealous?"

Taylor snorted. "No way! He's a stuck-up jerk."

"Yeah, and he'll be driving a 'Vette while your dad won't let you get your license." Nick muttered to himself while he pulled the clothes out of his suitcase and dumped them on the bed.

Taylor's childhood buddy knew him too well. Still, he was not jealous of Luke, even if he did get to drive a Corvette.

"There they are!" Nick lifted his swim trunks from the pile of clothes beside the suitcase. "Give me a second to change and then we'll go back to your cabin."

Luke, Brady and Steven were all gone by the time Taylor returned to Spruce cabin. He changed, grabbed his towel, and hurried to the beach with Nick. They tossed their towels on the sand and started toward the water. One look at the diving raft stopped Taylor in his tracks.

"Aw, look who's out there on the raft."

Nick shaded his eyes from the sun.

"Claire?"

"No. Luke."

Nick looked sideways at him. "So, does that mean we're not going out there?"

"Fat chance. Last one there buys a snack from the Shack." Taylor ran into the water, dove headfirst and swam like shark bait until he reached the raft. He clung to the ladder, catching his breath while Nick caught up. "You owe me a bag of chips."

"No fair. You got a head start."

The raft swayed as Taylor climbed onto it. He stepped onto the surface as Luke performed a flip off the diving board. Claire and another girl sat on the raft's edge beside the board, legs dangling above the water, clapping their hands in appreciation for Luke's dive.

Taylor mounted the board, barely giving Luke time to get out of the way before he took a running leap off the end. Pulling himself into a ball, arms tight around his knees, he dropped into the lake. That splash should get the girls' attention.

Surfacing, he saw the girls had moved. "What's wrong? You're not afraid of a little water, are you?" He shook the hair away from his eyes, sending water droplets in an arc around him.

Claire glared at him from her perch on the diving board.

"Any idiot can do a cannonball." She turned her back to the water and balanced on her toes at the end of the board. Bounce, bounce. With the third bounce, she launched herself into the air and flipped over backward, her body slicing through the water like a sharp knife.

"You gonna let a girl show you up like that?" Nick razzed.

Before Taylor could respond, Claire called up to her friend. "I'm going back to the beach. It's getting a little crowded out here." Her friend jumped into the water and they swam toward the pier while Taylor climbed onto the raft.

Nick landed a playful punch to his arm. "She loves you as much as she did last year."

From a corner of the raft, Luke added, "I hear she's crazy about that rock star, Steven Miller." Taylor laughed, but Luke wasn't smiling. "Do you always make fun of people you've just met?"

Nick stepped onto the diving board. "Oh no, you're not that special. He makes fun of everyone, whether he's just met you or not."

Taylor gave Luke a fake smile. "Just trying to make you feel like one of the gang."

Luke's lip curled and his eyes narrowed. Taylor turned his back to him and, moments later, a splash told him Luke had left.

Nick positioned himself for a dive. "I don't think he liked our company."

Taylor mimicked Claire's voice. "Yeah, it was getting a little crowded out here."

WHOSE DUMB IDEA was it to make everyone in the cabin eat their first meal together? Steven was the only one Taylor knew from last year, and that was a little awkward after he'd flipped Steven's canoe in the Water Carnival last summer. He'd rather be sitting with Nick.

Ignoring the chatter around the table, Taylor scanned the dining hall for familiar faces. He spotted Brady and recognized a few others at the thirty or more round tables filling the cavernous room. With everyone talking, the noise was worse than the school lunchroom. There was Claire, her hands making wild motions as she spoke to the girls at her table.

A slower movement beside Claire caught his eye, a hand waving side to side. The smiling face behind it belonged to *Marissa?* At Claire's table?

The name of Jesus Christ escaped Taylor's lips.

One of the boys at his table jumped up. "Where? Is He here, too?" He looked all around. "I wanna see Him!" Luke and the other boys at the table laughed.

Even Harris smiled, despite the serious tone of his voice. "That name deserves more respect. Don't be using it carelessly like that."

Taylor grimaced and hung his head. Chewed out by the counselor already, and in front of everyone else, too. This could be a long week. He tossed his hair back and caught Luke's scornful smirk. *Enough.* Taylor shoved back his chair, picked up his tray and went to find Nick.

On their way back to the cabins, a group of girls crossed their path. One waved and Nick waved back. A silly-looking grin stretched across Nick's face from one ear to the other.

"Who's that?" Taylor asked.

Nick's gaze followed the girls. "Her name's Alexis. She goes by Alex. She was behind me at check-in." Still grinning, he called to the girls. "Where're you going?"

Alex flashed a smile. "Down by the lake. 'Wanna come?"

"Sure!" Nick backhanded Taylor in the gut and whispered, "Meet you in chapel, near the back." He jogged to catch up with Alex and her friends.

Taylor huffed and stared after Nick. Now what was he supposed to do? His friend disappeared down the hillside to the lake. This week would really stink if Nick hung out with his girlfriend the whole time.

Taylor trudged on toward the cabin until a roaring engine interrupted his thoughts. The sound didn't last long enough to tell exactly where it came from. He stopped and listened. Another throaty rumble sent him hurrying toward the parking lot. It couldn't be Luke's 'Vette; his dad would have taken that home by now. Besides, this sounded too rough. Must be some other car.

At the edge of the parking lot, Taylor stopped and studied the few remaining cars. Most of the vehicles probably belonged to counselors and staff members. None looked capable of producing the sound he'd heard. He cocked an ear and listened again.

Another roar, louder and longer this time from the white shed off to the left of the lot. He'd seen the building before but never gave it much thought. A forest green pickup with Rustic Knoll's emblem on the door was parked in front of one of the three garage doors lining the front. The other two overhead doors were open, revealing a tractor in the middle bay and a much smaller grille peeking out from the near end. That must be the source of the rumble. Heart racing, Taylor sauntered up to the bay where a car's hood stood open in a toothless yawn. A man in brown uniform shirt and pants leaned over the engine.

Taylor peered into the garage, then sidled up to the car. He coughed. "Sweet car. Mind if I look?"

The man's head came up and he gave a friendly nod. He wiped his hand on a cloth rag, motioning for Taylor to look around. "You like?" His Spanish accent fit the deep chestnut brown of his face and arms. He wasn't much taller than Taylor, but he was stocky and his hair would soon be more white than black.

"It's awesome. I love cars." Taylor ran his hand across the left fender, the new red paint smooth beneath his fingertips. One wide black stripe bordered by narrow stripes ran from front to back atop the raised hood. Another thin stripe raced along the side of the car, from the Mach 1 lettering behind the front wheel to the rear wheel well. He bent down and stuck his head through the open passenger window. Compared to modern cars, the dashboard instruments looked small and simple. The seat covers, though tattered and ragged, beckoned him inside. Taylor resisted, moving on toward the back. His palm slid easily along the fastback down to the spoiler. Dual exhaust pipes peeked from beneath the bumper.

The man stepped off to the side, using the rag to wipe oil off the dipstick. "Is nice, eh?"

Taylor joined him, drinking in the sight of the old Mustang.

"It's really nice! What year?"

"1970."

"Can I sit in it?"

"Si! Yes." Taylor pulled the door open and slid onto the driver's seat, ignoring the foam that bulged through the fabric. His fingers curled around the narrow steering wheel. He closed his eyes, pressing his sandaled foot ever so lightly against the gas pedal. He itched to stomp on it, to hear the roar of the engine going full out. In his mind's eye, he watched the speedometer's needle push past 80, 90, 100.

Taylor opened his eyes and leaned his head out the open window. "Have you driven it yet?"

The man replaced the dipstick, then replied, "Is not quite ready." He came over and leaned his forearms on the window. "You drive?" His hands made steering motions.

"Not yet. I'm only fifteen. Next year, I get my license." As if that might actually happen. Taylor leaned his head back against the seat.

"Someday, you have a car like this, no?"

Taylor ran his hand across the instruments on the dash and let it fall to the gearshift. "I'd love a car like this." He gripped the wheel again and imagined speeding around a track, the sidelines a blur, engine revving until his teeth rattled. The man watched him with an understanding smile.

Taylor savored the dream a moment longer before dropping his hands to his lap, then reached for the door handle. The man stepped back allowing Taylor to get out and shut the door.

"Your name?"

"Taylor."

"Nice to meet you, Taylor." He put his hand out to shake. "I am Roberto Rodriguez. You know my wife, Juanie?"

Wa-nee? Taylor shook his head. How would he know this old guy's wife? "Oh! You mean Janie?"

Roberto's smile widened. "Si. Yes, she is cook."

"Sure, everyone knows Janie. I've seen you around, mowing the grass and stuff, but I didn't know you and Janie were married." Taylor took one more look at the Mustang and crossed his arms, sliding his hands into his armpits. "Thanks for letting me check out the car. It's really cool."

Roberto tipped his head sideways. "You come again. Maybe you help?"

Taylor shook the hair from his eyes for a clear view of Roberto's face. "Seriously? You'd let me work on it?"

"Si. You know about cars—engines, changing out seats, carpet?"

"I know a little about engines, but nothing about restoring a car." Taylor looked the car over again, his eyes wide. "How much work did you have to do on this?"

Roberto crooked a finger at him. "Come. I show you pictures."

3

Roberto pulled a three-ring binder from the shelf above his workbench, grabbed a small cooler and set it outside in the evening sunlight.

"You want a drink?" He flipped open the cooler to reveal cans of iced soda.

Not much variety—the man must like root beer. Taylor helped himself to a can and popped the top open.

Roberto took one as well, closed the lid and invited Taylor to sit on the cooler. He placed a metal folding chair speckled with dirt and paint next to Taylor, sat down and opened the binder. It had a battered look to it, like Taylor's notebook at the end of a school year. But the pictures inside were better than any algebra equations or sentence diagrams. The first page protector held an 8"x10" photo of the car sitting on blocks, its wheels missing. Dents marred the body in several spots, and its red paint looked faded and dull. A crack split the windshield. Rust clung to the fenders around the wheel wells.

Taylor turned the page. An inside shot showed the torn seat covers, the vinyl peeling away from the foam cushions, and a sagging headliner. One handle for raising and lowering the window was missing. The next several pages showed before and after shots of the engine parts—dirty and worn, then restored and looking like new.

Roberto leaned closer, adding his comments.

"I look for engine I can overhaul, keep original. No replace." He shook his finger.

Taylor looked up from the pictures. "How can you tell it's the original?"

"The number." He pointed to a picture showing numbers cast onto the engine block. "They match the car number. You know the VIN?"

Taylor nodded. "The vehicle identification number."

"Si. If engine is changed, numbers do not match."

"Is that important? I mean, if you can't tell except by checking the numbers, what's the difference?"

Roberto took a sip of his root beer, then tipped his head sideways and pressed his lips together. His fingers rubbed the late day stubble on his cheek then he pointed to Taylor's chest. "Is like your heart. The one you are born with works best for your body, si? You can replace it, but the body rejects it, no?" He shifted his weight on the chair. "Engine is heart of the car. So, I keep original. Clean it, repair it. I know what makes the car run." He pointed to his temple, then his chest. "I know its heart."

Sounds kinda hokey, but yeah, I get it.

Taylor flipped through more pictures of the engine going back into its compartment, and the body in various stages of repair and painting. At last, he closed the binder and handed it back to Roberto.

"Thanks. It's cool seeing what it looked like before."

Happy shouts and shrieks sounded from somewhere near the dining hall. Roberto checked his watch. "I keep you too long. You go?"

Taylor made no move to get up. "They're just playing some

stupid game to make sure we all get to know each other. If it's okay with you, I'd rather stay here."

A smile creased Roberto's weathered face. "Is okay with me." He put away the photo album then went to stand by the engine again. "You help?"

Taylor's comment to Dad about no cars at camp crossed his mind. He bit his tongue to keep from laughing out loud. If Dad only knew! He jumped up and stood beside Roberto.

I'd give just about anything to own a Mustang like this.

But without a driver's license, that would be pointless. He'd need to stay out of trouble, which meant keeping Marissa out of trouble. And that was next to impossible.

THE BAND HAD ALREADY STARTED their first song when Taylor slipped into the chapel. He spotted Nick in the middle of a row near the back and squeezed past the other kids. His buddy shouted over the music.

"'Bout time you got here. Where've you been?" Nick leaned away, his attention fastened on the front of the chapel.

Taylor shivered with excitement. "I've been working on a 1970 Mach I Mustang." He pronounced the name precisely.

Nick clearly did not believe him. "Where'd you find one of those?" His gaze shifted to the other side of the aisle.

"That shed out by the parking lot. You know the guy we see mowing the grass and stuff? That's Janie's husband. He's restoring this old Mustang out there where they keep the camp tractor and pickup. It's awesome."

"Does it run?" Despite his questions, Nick seemed distracted. He kept looking across the aisle.

"Yeah, it runs. He said I could help him work on it every night after supper." Taylor followed Nick's line of sight a few rows up and to the left. Alex. His buddy had fallen hard for this girl.

A drop of sweat slid down Taylor's spine, tickling as it went. Fans hanging from the ceiling's apex might have cooled things off if they rotated faster. The high ceiling of the chapel's A-frame did little to draw the heat up and away from a room crammed with teenagers bouncing to the music's rhythm. But he couldn't get into this kind of music no matter what the temperature. It was almost as boring as the hymns they sang in church back home. Now, if they played screamo music, that would be really cool.

The band finished and everyone sat down. While Zeke climbed onto the stage, a counselor moved a small table to the center and set a fancy, decorated box on top. The box sparkled with colored stones and glitter. Zeke dragged his easel with the pad of paper nearer to the box. The camp director's short nickname fit him better than his proper name, Rev. Zacharias. His stature along with his white hair made him easily recognizable around camp.

Taylor sank further into his seat. Not really hiding, but he'd spent way too much time in Zeke's office last year. Tipping Brady, Steven and Claire out of their canoe. The fight with Brady. He couldn't exactly blame that trouble on Marissa. He might need to make a small change here and there if he wanted his license.

Zeke removed the cover from his box of artist's chalk. "Who can tell me what it means to say someone has 'opened Pandora's box'?" Someone up in front answered and Zeke repeated it for everyone to hear.

"According to Greek mythology, Pandora was the first woman on earth. When she married, she received a large jar with instructions not to open it under any circumstances. But Pandora always wondered what was in that jar."

Zeke selected a piece of chalk and drew several green streaks on the paper, then stepped aside and drew the campers' attention to the box on the table. "Later generations have changed the jar to a box. Attractive, don't you think?"

Someone shouted, "What's in it?"

Others echoed the question and Zeke held up his forefinger. "Ah, you're curious, aren't you?"

A chorus of voices answered, "Yes!"

"Well, so was Pandora." He chose a different color chalk and went back to drawing the picture. "Eventually, her curiosity got the best of her. She only meant to take a peek. Thought she'd open it just enough to see what was inside and then close it again. Unfortunately, as soon as she lifted the cover from the jar, all kinds of evil escaped and spread over the whole earth." Zeke moved to the box and laid his hand on the lid. "Should I open it?"

Most of the campers cried yes; a few yelled no. Taylor sat up straight to see what Zeke would do. *Probably nothing in there. He's just playing it up to keep us interested.*

Zeke removed his hand, leaving the box unopened, and moved back to his easel.

"This myth is a perfect lead-in to the question I want us to consider this week. While you wonder about what might be in the box, I want you to think about what's in your heart. The Bible has a lot to say about the things we carry in our heart. For example, Jesus tells us in Matthew 6:21 that wherever our treasure is, that's where our heart will be. Our affections will be caught up in whatever we value and spend time on. In another place, Jesus said whatever comes out of our mouth reveals what's in our heart."

A pine tree took shape on Zeke's pad of paper, looking a lot like the tree outside Taylor's cabin. But now he was adding little red circles, like balls, to the tree. *Christmas? In July?*

Zeke put away his chalk and faced the campers. "Who knows what kind of tree this is?"

Several campers called it a Christmas tree, but Zeke shook his head. Others guessed pine or spruce but Zeke rejected every answer. Finally, he asked, "Doesn't anyone recognize an apple tree?"

Protests erupted, and campers called out their arguments.

"No way. That's not an apple tree."

"Apple trees have leaves, not needles."

"Apples don't grow on pine trees."

Zeke argued back. "What do you mean? Haven't you ever heard of *pine*apples?"

Taylor groaned along with the rest. "Okay, that was a bad joke." Zeke chuckled. "But you just proved my point. You don't expect to find apples on pine trees. Do grapes ever grow on a rose bush? Or flowers on an oak tree? Of course not. What if you went to the water fountain for a drink and dirty water came out of the spout? Would that surprise you?"

Zeke picked up his Bible and stepped off the stage into the aisle. "In Luke 6, Jesus reminds his followers that trees are recognized by their fruit. Good trees don't bear bad fruit and bad trees don't bear good fruit. In the same way, he says, 'A good man brings good things out of the good stored up in his heart. And an evil man brings evil out of the evil stored up in his heart. For the mouth speaks what the heart is full of.'"

The camp director paced the aisle, hands behind his back. "Let that thought sink in. Out of your mouth come the things that are in your heart." He returned to the front and faced them again.

"If your mouth is a water fountain, are you putting out sweet water that nourishes those around you? Or is it disgusting, foul water that people avoid? Do your words encourage others and build them up, or do you tear them down?" He held a fist over his heart. "You only get two choices. Good or evil. There's no in-between."

Zeke raised a hand toward his drawing. "Bad trees can't produce good fruit. If you're filling your heart with dark stuff, don't expect your words to be light and uplifting. But if you store up good things in your heart, you don't have to worry how your words will affect others. James, the brother of Jesus, called the tongue a fire, a restless evil full of deadly poison."

That verse sounded familiar. Zeke had Taylor read it out loud in his office last summer after the fight with Brady.

The director climbed back onto the stage and stood near his drawing. "The tongue can only speak what is in the heart. You have an assignment for tomorrow. Between now and our next evening worship, listen to yourself. Pay attention to what comes out of your mouth. Is it sweet or sour? Garbage or good? Discover what's in your heart by listening to what comes out of your mouth. We'll leave the box up here as a reminder. And each evening, we'll talk about what we might find when we look inside."

If my heart is where my treasure is, it must be in the garage with that Mustang.

TAYLOR LEFT Nick to flirt with Alex and sucked in the cooler air outside the chapel. He hurried to the cabin and pulled out his magazine. It had regained its appeal since he'd been with Roberto. He flipped through the pages until he found a 1970 Mach 1 Mustang like Roberto's. The picture didn't do it justice. Taylor held the magazine beside his bed to look at it in better light.

Luke wandered over, toothbrush in hand. "Pony cars." He said it like he'd just found horse manure on his shoe.

Taylor pulled the magazine to his chest. "What's your problem? Pony cars are cool."

Luke wiped his mouth with the towel slung around his neck. "Corvettes are cool. Pony cars are just pony cars. Like ponies on a merry-go-round. They're for kids."

Harris interrupted, calling everyone for devotions. Luke tossed his toothbrush across Steven's bed onto his own and made his way into the common room. Taylor stuffed the magazine under his pillow. He'd look at it again when "Puke" wasn't around.

The comfortable armchairs had all been claimed and Taylor wasn't about to squeeze into the spot beside Luke on the sofa. He dropped to the floor near the front door. The cabin was almost as warm as the chapel had been, but occasionally a cool draft filtered through the screen door and wafted over his legs.

Harris looked around the group, checking names on a list in his lap and matching them with the faces around the room. He ran through a short review of camp and cabin rules—no swimming without a buddy, no noise or leaving the cabin after lights out—then repeated Zeke's question of the week. "What's in your heart?"

Taylor kept his eyes averted, like most of the other guys trying to avoid answering the question. Finally, someone spoke up. "That's kind of a girly question."

Harris pursed his lips and appeared to be thinking. "Okay. What's in your gut? What is it that makes you do the things you do and say the things you say? Is it ego? Fear? Anger?"

Steven raised his hand. "Does it have to be negative?"

"Good question. No, there could be positive things like love, courage, selflessness, faith." Harris waited, his gaze traveling around the room. No one else spoke. "Each night this week, Zeke will talk about different things we might find in our heart, or in our gut, if we take the time to look close and be honest. Don't just blow it off. Think about it. Be honest with yourself. You might find you have some decent things inside. Or you might discover it's more like Pandora's box, full of evil, disgusting stuff. If that's the case, let's spend this week of camp working on changing that."

Taylor jumped to his feet the moment Harris finished praying. He hurried to brush his teeth, then pulled off his t-shirt and dropped it on top of his duffle bag. He hopped into bed, turning his back to the Puke-ster and the guys chatting it up on the other side of the bunkroom.

Opening his magazine, he turned to the next to last page of photos. Was it even worth dreaming about a car like Roberto's? If he had his driver's license, he could get a job, save enough to buy a car he could fix up like Roberto was doing. Dad should be happy with that—a job and a car to work on would keep him out of trouble. If only he could make Dad see it that way.

4

Taylor met Nick at his cabin the next morning and they headed for the dining hall. The sticky sweet aroma of pancakes and syrup laced the air, and Taylor's mouth watered. A small crowd of kids surrounded the announcement board at the Snack Shack as they neared the dining hall. Taylor stopped, backhanding Nick's arm. "Maybe they put us on the same Rec team this year."

Nick grunted. "That'll never happen. Don't you know Zeke watches to see who's hanging out together so he can make sure they're on different teams?" He craned his neck to see the board from the back of the crowd while Taylor pushed through to the front, earning a sour look from Claire when he moved up next to her.

Marissa called from somewhere behind him. "Taybo! Look at my team and tell me if you know anyone."

He flinched at the use of his pet name, especially when Claire arched an eyebrow at him. Her lips formed the word—Taybo? She barely suppressed a dimpled grin, and turned back to the board.

Ignoring her, Taylor studied the posted lists until he found his name. He scanned the other names on his team. There had to be a few he knew from last year. None sounded familiar, except one.

Blue eyes met his as he turned to look at her. *Claire Thompson.* She wrinkled her nose and with a groan, pushed her way out from the crowd of campers. No matter what she thought of him, being on Claire's team was a good thing. Athletic and competitive, she never wimped out like a lot of girls.

Nick moved up beside him and, after looking over the lists, he turned a full-on grin toward Taylor. "Alex is on my team."

Before Taylor could respond, Marissa nudged him from the other side. Having taken over Claire's spot, she leaned in to him. "Did you look at my team? Is there anyone good?"

Taylor found her name and read through the others on her team. He moaned at the names he recognized. "Your team is stacked. You guys are gonna kill everyone."

Rissa clapped and bounced on her toes. "Really?"

Besides the familiar names from last year, Taylor recognized another one on Rissa's list. But he wasn't about to tell her Luke-puke was on her team. Let her find that out on her own.

THE REC SCHEDULE listed Wheel Steal for his team's organized game after lunch. Taylor made his way down to what used to be the volleyball court behind the clinic. Since last summer, a new volleyball court had been built with a sand base. What remained of the old site was mostly dirt, the grass on both ends having long ago surrendered to the continual trampling from hundreds of teenage feet. Today, dozens of inflated inner tubes lay in a jumbled line where the net used to hang and the whole area had been watered down enough to resemble a giant mud pit.

Taylor wandered about one end with the rest of his team. Claire ignored him, chatting with some of the other kids like they were old friends. He checked out the team at the opposite end and caught sight of Marissa waving to him.

Seriously? Playing the stacked team on the first day?

Then again, he'd be playing against Luke-puke. He'd have a chance to see what the Pukester was made of.

Harris jogged up and blew his whistle. "Who's ready to get down and dirty?"

A few guys roared their approval. Some moans came from the girls.

Harris displayed a fake-looking frown. "Ladies, you can't let these guys have all the fun. Don't you remember making mud pies when you were little? This is just like that. Almost."

The girls bunched together, casting doubtful looks at the muddy field.

"Can I go back to the cabin and change?" asked one. "My mom will kill me if I get these white shorts all dirty."

Harris cocked his head. "Girl, haven't you heard of detergent and washing machines? And bleach?" He blew his whistle again. Clearly, the girls were not thrilled about this game. Even Claire grimaced.

Taylor glanced at his shorts and t-shirt. No problem. He'd go jump in the lake after they were done.

From mid-field near the pile of inner tubes, Harris shouted to both teams. "Welcome to Wheel Steal. Your goal for this game is to grab the most inner tubes, or wheels, and get them back to your starting line. At my signal, each team member will run to the center, grab as many tubes as you can and run them back."

Someone from the other team asked a question. "Can we roll them or do we have to carry them?"

"Any way you like. Just get them back to your starting line." Harris pointed to the opposite ends of the mud field. "If two of you from opposing teams grab the same wheel, whoever gets it across their line first gets to keep it, even if the opposing team member is still attached. However, stealing wheels from the other team's starting line is illegal and you will be arrested and thrown in jail. Any questions?"

One girl raised her hand. "Does everybody on the team have to do this?"

"That's up to you and your team. But if they lose because you stood and watched, remember you will be playing with these same people every day for the rest of the week." When no one else asked any more questions, Harris called, "Okay, line up across your starting line."

Taylor kicked off his flip-flops and assumed a runner's stance at the starting line. With Claire next to him, he couldn't resist a little teasing. "Not worried about a little mud, are you?"

Claire raised one eyebrow. "Not me. I bet I can grab more wheels than you."

Taylor grinned. "You're on."

Harris blew the whistle and Taylor raced for the tubes. Mud squished between his toes and splattered his ankles. Twice, his feet nearly slid out from under him, but he reached the middle, grabbed two inner tubes and tried a skating motion on the way back, using the slippery mud to his advantage. After tossing the tubes across his goal line, he headed back for more and met Claire. One of her arms skewered two tubes through the center while her other hand clutched a third. Her forearms and legs were smeared with mud.

Taylor growled to himself. Already one tube behind and the game had just begun. He pulled two from the jumble in the center and slipped his left arm through the middle like Claire had done. He yanked on another one but Marissa pulled from the other side.

"Let go, Taybo! I got it first."

"Nope, it's mine." Taylor pulled again but Marissa held on with both hands. He relaxed for only a moment then tugged hard. Marissa lost her balance and stumbled toward him, still clinging to the tube. She dropped to her knees in the mud and

Taylor dragged her several yards before Luke came to her rescue.

Grabbing onto the tube, Luke held it steady while Marissa regained her footing. Mud stuck to her legs in globs, but together, she and Luke pulled the tube past the center and on toward their goal.

Taylor dug his heels into the ground to keep from being dragged along, but it did no good. The inner tube worked itself loose from his grip, slipping through his mud-covered hands. No way was he letting Luke win this one. He dropped the two tubes on his other arm and adjusted his grip on the disputed one. He almost fell backward when Marissa let go of the tube.

She ran to his side and grabbed the tubes he'd dropped. "Luke! Catch."

Luke released the disputed tube, caught the one Marissa tossed and they both hustled back to their goal, leaving Taylor sitting in the mud with one lousy tube. He'd landed on his backside when Luke let go, splattering mud onto his shoulders and head.

Taylor swiped his face, but his muddy hands only made it worse. Dirt grit leaked through the corners of his mouth, crunching when he clenched his teeth. All around him, campers screamed, shouted, grabbed tubes and dragged them back to their starting lines. But the noise didn't drown out Claire's familiar laughter.

"You'll never beat me sitting around like that." With one tube on her left arm, she reached for Taylor's tube, now lying in the mud beside him. She turned to race back to the starting line, but Taylor grabbed her foot, sending her sprawling in the mud. The inner tubes flew out to her sides, splattering mud in every direction.

Taylor howled at the sight of her mud-covered cheeks and the chocolate-colored clumps of dirt that clung to her blonde hair.

Rising to his knees, he mimicked her voice. "You'll never beat me lying around like that."

Claire snarled. "We're supposed to be on the same team, you idiot." She pushed herself to a sitting position, scooped up a handful of mud and flung it at him.

Taylor's raised arm only partially succeeded in shielding his face. He returned the volley. Claire turned away, but not soon enough. The mud ball hit the side of her head and dripped down her hair onto her ear, neck and shoulder. Chin jutting out, eyes narrowed, she dug her fingers into the mud.

Harris's whistle blasted. "Taylor, you're out. Your girlfriend, too. You two come sit here on the sideline until you learn how to play nice."

Claire moaned.

Taylor protested. "What? No way. My team needs me."

Harris spoke around the whistle clenched between his teeth. "Shoulda thought of that before you tripped your girlfriend."

"I'm not his girlfriend." Claire jumped up from the mud and kicked at the tubes she'd been carrying. She peeled away the bangs plastered to her forehead, scraped the mud from her hands and shuffled to the sideline where she dropped to the grass with a huff. Her shoulders rose and fell with every breath and she pointedly ignored Taylor.

Taylor followed her to the sideline, keeping distance between them, and sank to the ground. Every square inch of his shorts and shirt were dirt brown. He peeled the wet cloth away from his skin. Luke would pay for this. If he hadn't come to Rissa's aid and let go of the tube, Taylor would still be in the game. But the memory of Marissa's mud covered legs and Claire's belly-flop brought a grin to his face. *Worth every speck of dirt.*

The game continued a few more minutes. When all the tubes had been moved to one side or the other, Harris counted and declared Luke and Marissa's team the winner.

Who cares? The mud on Taylor's body and clothing was

drying and becoming stiff. As soon as Harris dismissed them, he headed across the camp to the lake.

Outside the dining hall, Roberto was painting some kind of narrow wooden platform that rose several feet above the ground. He laughed when he saw Taylor. "Wheel Steal?"

"Yeah. I'm going to the lake to wash off." Taylor detoured over to where Roberto was working. He'd seen that structure last year but hadn't noticed any use for it. "What is that?"

Roberto drew his brush along one of the supporting legs. "Is for a bell, to wake you up and call to meals, Bible study."

"How come you're painting it if there's no bell?"

"New bell is coming."

"What happened to the old one?"

"Stolen. Last summer."

"Who would steal a bell?"

Roberto shrugged. "Police say is probably kids living around lake. Maybe a summer home." He pointed his paintbrush at the lake. "They come late at night, by boat. Take bell and leave. Must have been two, maybe three. Bell was iron. Heavy." He flexed his arms in a muscle-builder pose.

"So, when's the new bell going up?" Taylor looked to the top.

Roberto dipped his brush into the white paint. "Tomorrow." Before he touched the brush to the tower's leg, he eyeballed Taylor from head to toe. "You go wash?"

Taylor glanced at his dirty hands, arms, legs and feet. "Yeah, I better get going or I won't be able to move when all this dries. See ya later."

"Tonight?" Roberto held his paintbrush up in a kind of salute.

"Yeah! I'll be there right after supper." No way he'd miss the best part of the day.

A SURPRISE PUNCH to the arm at supper almost sent ice water

spewing from Taylor's mouth. He managed to swallow it, but the water in his glass splashed all over his hand and dripped onto his lap. The glass thunked as he set it down. He raised a fist toward his attacker, but released it when he saw his sister.

"Rissa! What was that for?"

"You are so rude." She punched his arm again. "No wonder she practically ignored you. How do you expect to get a girlfriend if you treat her like that?"

Taylor twisted in his chair to see her better. "What are you talking about?"

"What you did to Claire. I am so embarrassed. How could you be so mean?" She crossed her arms and shifted to one leg while her other foot beat the floor.

Taylor grabbed a napkin and wiped off his arm. "She threw mud first."

"Yeah, after you tripped her so she fell on her face. In the mud. I apologized for you, but from now on, I expect you to treat her the way you treat me."

"And what happens if I don't?"

Marissa pressed her lips together, her eyes narrowing as she fixed him with an angry glare. Then, slowly, her mouth curled into a sly smile and her voice took on a sugary tone.

"If you don't, I tell Daddy all about it and you'll never get your license." She stuck out her tongue and flounced away.

The guys at the table hooted.

"Guess she told you." Nick laughed and slapped him on the back.

Taylor's cheeks grew warm. He shoved his chair back and stood up.

Nick looked up in surprise. "Where you going?"

"None of your business. Go hang out with Alex." Taylor grabbed his tray and hurried for the exit.

5

Taylor left the dining hall and headed for the machine shed. Marissa's chewing out in front of the guys still burned. She wouldn't really tell Dad. At least, she never had before. But he couldn't afford to take a chance. Not if he hoped to get his license any time before he graduated.

At the edge of the parking lot, his steps slowed to a stop. The shed was closed. None of the garage doors stood open, no sound. His breath left him and his shoulders sagged. *Where's Roberto? He said he'd be here.* Taylor curled his lip at the thought of playing the stupid all-camper games scheduled between supper and evening worship. If only there were a camp dedicated to cars, where guys could go and learn all about mechanics, maintenance, styles, speed. He'd love it, but of course Dad would never send him to a camp like that.

What should he do? Go back to the cabin? He took one last look just as a sudden squeaking and grinding signaled the opening of the shed's overhead doors. Roberto waved from inside and Taylor ran to join him. "I didn't think you were here."

Roberto motioned him inside. "I am here, like I promised. Tonight, we work on timing and carburetor." He tossed the key to

Taylor, who caught it in the air. Roberto lifted the hood. "Start it for me?"

Taylor hadn't started a car since that one time when Jesse let him drive around the parking lot of an abandoned shopping center. What a kick to bring this machine to life, and he didn't even have to ask! He sank into the driver's seat, rested one foot against the accelerator, fitted the key into the ignition, and braced himself for the engine's roar. He turned the key. The engine coughed and went silent.

Roberto peeked around the side of the hood. "Push pedal to the floor, then let up. Try again." He twisted his wrist like he was turning the key.

Taylor followed the instructions and this time, the engine rumbled to life. The seat vibrated beneath him. *Feels like it can't wait to get loose and cruise the roads.*

Calling for Taylor to join him, Roberto leaned over the engine and pointed. He had to shout over the engine noise. "You work on these before?"

"Some."

Liar. He hadn't actually worked on them, but he'd watched when Jesse and his friends tinkered with their cars. This engine, with all the wires, carburetor and everything exposed, looked different from the modern engines. Exhaust swirled around them, dangerous if not for the open bay doors.

"Listen." Roberto bobbed his head and shoulders in time with the engine's throbbing. "Rough. You hear?"

The sound pulsed in Taylor's chest, the jerky quality Roberto indicated.

"Is too much gas in carburetor." He handed Taylor a screwdriver and pointed to a spot near the bottom of the engine. His hands made a twisting motion then he pointed to his ear and motioned for Taylor to begin.

Taylor reached down, and dropped the screwdriver. It clattered against the engine and hit the floor beneath the car. So much for looking like he knew what he was doing. "Sorry."

Roberto bent down and reached under the car to retrieve the tool then handed it back to him.

"Is no problem. Try again."

This time, Taylor held tight as he fitted the screwdriver's head into a screw about the size of a pencil's eraser. Gripping the handle with both fists, he gave it a slight twist. The engine evened out to a steady rumble. Roberto moved his index finger in a circle, and Taylor turned the screw farther. The engine sputtered and almost died. He looked to Roberto, whose finger now circled in the opposite direction. Taylor switched direction, twisting the screwdriver slowly until the engine returned to an even hum.

Roberto clapped him on the back and took the screwdriver from him. "Good!"

Taylor stood a little taller and slung the hair back from his eyes. Jesse's friends used to talk about adjusting the idle on their cars, but they'd never let him close enough to see exactly what they were doing. He'd bet his monthly allowance Luke had never done anything like this. Luke's dad probably made enough money to hire any mechanic he wanted, but did Luke even know how to check the oil? The guy had probably never lifted the hood of one of his fancy Corvettes.

Roberto handed Taylor something that looked like a ray gun from an old science fiction movie. They worked on adjusting the timing and made other tweaks to the engine. When they finally shut off the car, the noise from the other campers engaged in the evening game reached their ears.

Roberto tipped his head toward the voices. "You no want to play?"

"Naw. Those games are stupid. I'd much rather do this." Taylor jerked his thumb toward the car. He itched to see how it performed on the road. "When can we take it for a drive?"

Roberto shook his head. "Is not ready to drive."

He put away the tools and offered Taylor a drink from his cooler. The garage had grown especially warm with the car's exhaust. Taylor accepted the soda and followed Roberto outside where the evening was beginning to cool down. He opened the can and gulped down half the cold drink, but couldn't control the belch that followed.

The older man didn't seem to mind. Roberto clapped him on the shoulder. "You are good student." His smile wrinkled the tanned, leathery skin around his eyes. He tapped his ear. "You will be good mechanic. Like musician, you hear the music of the engine."

Taylor chuckled. He was no musician, but the analogy made him smile. Car engines did sound like music to him. Some were loud and powerful, like his screamo tunes. Others were smooth as elevator music. If only Dad understood him like Roberto. But Dad never said anything positive, even after he'd raised that D in Algebra up to a B+.

Roberto set up his folding chair. "You take driving class?"

Taylor's hair fell over his face as he bent to sit down on the cooler. "I hope so. I turn 16 next February. I can't wait to drive."

"You have brothers? Sisters?"

"One of each. My brother's older, but my sister's here at camp. She's only thirteen." He braced for an embarrassing question about his brother then decided to change the subject before it came. "Do you have kids?"

Roberto held up two fingers, then three, then one. "Two boys, three girls. And one grandchild almost here. My oldest daughter is due soon. Any day." He raised his soda, as if in a toast. "I be abuelo!"

Taylor raised his can as well. "You'll make a great grampa. Do your sons like cars?"

The older man took a sip of soda and smacked his lips. "They play soccer, baseball. No time for cars."

Irony. That's what his English teacher would call it. Roberto loved cars, but his sons were athletes. Taylor loved cars, but Dad's a coach. Why does that happen?

Taylor looked back at the Mustang. "How long before you can drive it?"

Roberto pursed his lips. "Still has much work to do. You come back tomorrow?"

"Yeah. Sure." Not very enthusiastic. Where's the fun in working on a car if you can't take it out for a spin, see how it works? Still, he'd learned more in one hour with Roberto than he'd ever learned hanging around Jesse and his friends. And Roberto actually seemed to like having him around. "I'll be here every night."

Roberto nodded. "Good. Tomorrow, we change carpet, maybe seat covers." He got up and stowed the cooler and chair in the garage. After locking the side door, he grabbed his hat and punched a button, then ducked out beneath the descending bay doors. "You go to worship now?"

Taylor sighed and raked his fingers through his hair. "Yeah, I guess."

"You no like Pastor Zeke?"

"He's okay. I like his stories, but the rest of it's kind of boring. I'm not really into religious stuff."

Roberto seemed to chew on that. He took another swallow of soda. "You know God?"

"Yeah, I know all about God." Taylor shrugged. "But it doesn't seem like He's real interested in me, y'know? Cars are more interesting. They're exciting."

Roberto nodded again, studying his shoe as he scuffed the sole against the edge of the pavement. "You think maybe God is like car factory?"

Taylor frowned. "What do you mean?"

"He makes you, sends you out, but then He does not care what happens to you?"

"Yeah. Yeah, that's pretty close. I mean, unless you go kill someone or rob a bank. Then I think He cares."

Roberto finished the last of his soda and rolled the can between his palms. "Tonight, you listen to Zeke. Tomorrow, tell me what he say. Okay?"

"Okay."

Roberto waved goodnight and shuffled across the parking lot.

First, Dad tells him to listen to Zeke, and now Roberto. *Is there something I'm supposed to hear?* Taylor hurried to the chapel where he found Nick in the crush of campers. They squeezed through the doors and Taylor grabbed two seats near the back. Nick craned his neck, searching the crowd. Looking for Alex, no doubt.

Marissa and a friend sidled through the row in front of them. Resting one knee on the seat, Marissa leaned toward Taylor and Nick, smacking her gum. "Hi guys!"

Taylor returned her cheery look with one of disgust. "Riss, you're not going to sit there, are you?"

Her hands flew to her hips, elbows jutting out. "Fine! I'll just pretend I don't know you. It won't be hard."

She spun around and plopped down on the seat. Her gum popped louder, one snap after another.

Taylor rolled his eyes. He and Nick were here first. She should be the one to move.

Luke sauntered in and Marissa waved him over to the empty seat beside her. Before sitting down, Luke sent a smirk in Taylor's direction, as if his whole reason for sitting there was to annoy him.

A foul word formed in Taylor's mind and his gut burned when Marissa leaned into Luke's shoulder. How could he pay attention to Zeke with those two in front of him? They ignored the music and singing, and spent the whole time chatting and laughing instead.

At last, the band finished and Zeke took the stage, moving his easel and pad of drawing paper to the center. The jeweled box still sat on the table at center stage.

"Last night I asked you to think about what's in your heart. If we opened your heart, like Pandora opened her jar, what would come out of it? Did you listen to your words today? Some of you may have heard bad language, gossip or insults coming out of your mouth. Tonight, we'll talk about something else that might be in your heart. It's something that's not always wrong but can lead to serious consequences if given free reign." Zeke took a piece of chalk and sketched a house with vines growing up the walls.

Taylor leaned sideways to see around Luke's head. He stretched his legs and knocked over an empty water bottle left behind earlier in the day. The thin plastic crackled as Taylor caught it beneath his foot.

Marissa half-turned toward him. "Shh-hh!"

Taylor gave it one more crackle to show how little he cared what she thought.

Zeke turned from his sketch and faced the campers. "Pride is good when it motivates us to do our best, to take care of what God has given us. But if it's not balanced with humility, pride is a lot like the kudzu vine that grows in parts of the United States. Kudzu grows so fast it's often used to prevent soil erosion. It can feed livestock, its fibers can be used to make baskets, and it has some medicinal qualities. But if left to grow unhindered, it will cover everything in sight. Kudzu vines can overtake trees and vegetation, smothering them by shading out needed sunlight and eventually killing them.

"If we allow our pride to grow without any restrictions, it becomes arrogance. And arrogance endangers not only the one who possesses it, but also anyone who comes under its shadow."

Luke and Marissa whispered back and forth. Taylor leaned forward. "Shh-hh!" They both turned and glared at him.

Who cares? Luke's the one who should be listening to Zeke. He needs to hear this.

Zeke drew more vines over the house until they blocked the windows, the doorway, and covered the roof. Several tendrils reached for a nearby tree like bony fingers in a horror movie. "The Bible warns us, 'Pride goes before a fall.' A person who thinks they can't fail usually will at some point. After the Israelites moved into the Promised Land, they forgot that God had blessed them with houses they didn't build and crops they didn't plant. They took the credit for their prosperity, eventually rejecting God completely, and the nation of Israel became slaves to the Assyrians and the Babylonians."

Taylor shifted in his seat. That was all ancient history. *What does it have to do with us?*

As if in answer to the question, Zeke set his chalk down and faced the campers. "Now, let me give you a more recent example to show you how destructive pride and arrogance can be." He stepped down from the stage and paced down the aisle.

"Several years ago, a wealthy Colorado businessman was known for his arrogance. When he hired someone to do a job for him, if he thought the job should be done a certain way, even an expert couldn't convince him to do it differently. It had to be done his way, because he knew bestor so he thought.

"This man owned a small airplane that he used for business. But he also enjoyed flying for fun, soaring over the mountains outside of Denver to enjoy the beautiful scenery."

Zeke reached the back of the room, turned and made his way toward the front. "One day, this man took his twelve year-old grandson and another friend for a ride in his plane. They went up late in the afternoon and by the time they returned, it was dark. As they were coming in for a landing, the control tower radioed him a warning that he was coming in too low and needed to increase his altitude. But the arrogant man thought he knew better than the tower operator and flew his plane right into a hill-side, killing himself, his grandson, and his friend."

Taylor blinked. Only an occasional shuffle of sandals on the floor broke the silence that blanketed the room.

"What's in your heart?" Zeke asked. "If it's unbridled pride or arrogance, get rid of it. Don't let it affect you or those you love."

Dad will make sure I don't get arrogant, but I sure hope Luke was listening.

6

Zeke's dismissal sent campers into the aisle, blocking Taylor's exit. He had to get away from Marissa and Luke. Every time Luke bent down to whisper in her ear, her giggles made bile creep up Taylor's throat. He imagined lots of things Luke might be saying and none of them were good.

Luke wedged himself into the aisle. Leading Marissa by the hand, he elbowed his way to the door. She waved to Taylor on her way out. "G'night, Taybo!"

Taylor gritted his teeth. Tomorrow, he'd threaten her life if she used his nickname again. He'd warn her about getting so friendly with Luke, too.

When he finally made it back to the cabin, he pulled off his shirt and dropped it in the growing pile on his duffle bag. Auto magazine in hand, he stretched out on his bunk until Harris called his name.

"Taylor, you coming? We're waiting for you." The bunkroom had emptied. His cabin mates, laughing and joking, were all gathered in the common room for devotions. Taylor jumped from the bed to join them.

Crack! Searing pain exploded in his little toe after it smacked against the steel frame of his bed. A foul word shot from his mouth. He grabbed his foot and hopped into the common room, falling onto the nearest sofa where he nearly landed in Steven's lap.

Harris winced. "Oh, man, I know that hurt."

Understatement of the year.

The counselor looked around the room. "Who's missing?"

Catching his breath against the pain, Taylor glanced around at the other guys. *Luke?* His gut tightened. Wherever Luke was, Marissa was probably there, too. "Luke's still out. Want me to go look for him?"

He wasn't going anywhere with this toe, but it sure would be fun to sneak up on them.

Harris pulled out his cell phone. "It's okay. I've got it." He typed a message and slipped the phone back in his pocket. "The God Squad will find him."

"God Squad?" asked one of the guys. "What's that?"

"Not what. Who. Sometimes it's Zeke, but usually the maintenance guys make rounds after hours." Harris settled into his chair and opened his Bible. "I want to go back and talk some more about what Zeke said last night. And Taylor, I hope you don't mind if I use you as an example."

Did he have a choice? Taylor agreed and rubbed his throbbing toe.

"We just witnessed a great illustration of Zeke's lesson. What's in your heart? Your gut? How do you react to something that's painful? What comes out of your mouth when you're hurting, either physically or emotionally?"

Taylor piped up. "It's not hallelujah, praise the Lord. That's for sure." Disrespectful, yeah, but his toe was killing him. He wasn't going to worry what came out of his mouth.

Harris didn't seem to take offense. "I don't expect an immediate spiritual response to pain. I'm talking about how we tend to act one way when people are watching compared to when they aren't watching. Most of us control our language. We avoid picking our nose and other things we don't want people to see us doing. It's when no one's looking, or when something shocks us —those unguarded moments that tell you what's really in your gut."

The counselor flipped some pages in his Bible. "This is the passage Zeke talked about last tonight, where Jesus is speaking to the Pharisees, the religious leaders of the day. They kept a strict code of behavior so everyone would be impressed with their righteousness. Outwardly, they kept all the rules, but Jesus saw that their hearts were full of jealousy, hatred and anger. They'd point fingers and accuse anyone who didn't live up to their outward standard of perfection. But Jesus called them white-washed tombs— looking good on the outside while their hearts were dead."

Sounds like Dad. He wanted everyone to think he was the perfect coach with the perfect team. But when Jesse missed that pass that cost them the state championship, the things that came out of Dad's mouth were nowhere near perfect.

Steven leaned over and whispered. "How's it feel? Any better?"

"Not much. I think I broke it."

"I believe it. Man, I know how that hurts. Done it a zillion times."

"Tonight," Harris continued, "I'm going to ask you guys to be totally honest. You won't get in any trouble. I'm not taking down names. But I want you to raise your hand if you've ever cussed or used a vulgar word. I'll be the first one." He lifted his hand above his head.

Taylor raised his hand, along with Steven and most of the other guys. The one or two who didn't raise their hands were probably lying.

Harris thanked them for being honest. "Now I've got another

question for you. If a girl uses bad language, does that make her more attractive or less?"

Taylor had to think about that one. Some of the girls at school cursed and used a lot of crude language. They liked being seen as tough, gritty, even boyish. But a lot of other girls used foul language, too. He'd never connected the way they talked with whether or not he found them attractive. Maybe that's what made Claire different. Even during Wheel Steal when he tripped her and she fell flat in the mud, she didn't cuss him out like most girls would have. Why not?

Harris continued. "If cussing and foul language makes a girl less attractive, why is it any different for us guys? We use words to make other guys think we're tough. But really, how tough do you have to be to say a simple cuss word? It's easy, right? Don't even have to think about it. What does that tell us about what's in our gut?" He paused for several moments before pointing toward the lake.

"You're able to swim in that lake because it's fed by springs. Good, clean water bubbling up out of the ground. But what if those springs started putting out some foul-smelling, poisonous water? Not all the time, but once or twice a day. Enough for you to notice the smell, the taste. Would you still swim in it?"

Harris leaned forward in his chair. "Listen, guys. Don't blow off Zeke's message. I really want you to think about this. Whatever is in your heart—your gut—whether it's healthy or contaminated can set the whole course of your life."

An image of Jesse in his prison cell sprang to Taylor's mind. Crude language didn't send his brother to jail, but was it a sign of the poison in his heart? Jesse had seemed like a great guy. Taylor and his friends all looked up to him, especially when he led the football team to the first state tournament in the school's history. He was a hero. Until he quit the team. He never said why, but he'd probably had enough of Dad's criticism. The other coaches recognized and celebrated Jesse's successes, but not Dad. All Dad saw were the mistakes. If Jesse'd heard one word of encouragement from Dad, he might have played his senior year, might have gone back and won the state tournament. But Dad wouldn't let him forget losing that one championship game. So Jesse turned in his uniform.

Was Dad's criticism the poison that filled Jesse's gut, prompting him to steal a car to embarrass Dad? Was that same poison now dripping into his own life? Maybe Dad was right and he'd end up in jail like Jesse. But if he did, whose fault would it be —his or Dad's?

Footsteps approached the door. It opened and someone ushered Luke in.

"Thanks, Paul," Harris called as the figure retreated. He waited for Luke to settle onto the floor, the only place left to sit. "Glad you could join us. Where've you been?"

"Just hanging with a friend." Luke shrugged, a lazy smile spreading across his face. He crossed his legs at the ankle and leaned back against the wall.

"Well, since you like being out after hours, you can expect an early wake-up call tomorrow morning. You'll be hanging with me while I run five miles."

Gasps echoed around the room. Luke's smile drooped, losing some of its cockiness.

Was Marissa the friend he was hanging with? Had he whispered an invitation to break curfew as they hurried out of chapel?

If Taylor had any hope of getting his license, he'd have to keep her out of trouble. Sometimes, her 'try anything once for fun' attitude made him laugh, but every time she got into trouble, he got blamed.

Harris finished devotions and dismissed them with a five-minute warning until lights out. With his toe still at a dull throb, Taylor stood and hobbled to his suitcase for his toothbrush, then limped to the bathroom and waited until a sink opened up. Usually, he elbowed someone aside, but tonight he didn't want to

risk anyone stepping on his toe. And he stayed well clear of the
bed frame on his way back to bed.

Harris turned the lights out and Taylor lay in bed, thinking
about Roberto and his Mustang, and Marissa and Luke. An idea
took shape. The perfect payback for Luke dropping him in the
mud. And if all went well, no one would connect him to
the crime.

THE SCREEN DOOR'S squeak roused Taylor from sleep. He struggled to open his eyes. Morning sunlight brightened the windows,
but everyone was still asleep. Well, almost everyone. He pushed
up on his elbow and peered across at Luke's bed. Empty. How
long does it take to run five miles? He'd need to hurry.

Stifling a yawn, he kicked back his sleeping bag and slipped
out of bed, arranging his bedding to look like he was still sleeping
there.

His shorts from yesterday lay in the heap on his duffle bag. He
pulled them on while rounding Steven's bed, stepping gingerly
around sneakers and suitcases to protect his injured toe. Without
a sound, he crept over to Luke's bunk. One leg of boxer shorts
with Corvettes on it stuck out from the corner of Luke's suitcase
under his bed. Taylor pulled out the boxers, stuffed them in his
pocket and hurried to the front door. Now, how to get out of here
without waking anyone else? He couldn't waste any time. Harris
and Luke would be back soon.

Using light pressure, Taylor opened the door just wide
enough for his slim frame to slip through. The squeak threatened, but he was outside and easing the door closed before it
could do any damage. With a quick check in every direction for
possible spies, Taylor leaped off the front step and dashed toward
the flagpole, ignoring the dull ache in his toe.

Sunlight filtered through the trees, dappling the ground. Dew chilled his bare feet and made the ground slippery, but at least the cold numbed his toe a bit. He neared the flagpole and hid behind a tree, scanning all around for witnesses.

The flagpole stood near the bell tower, a short distance from the dining hall. Out there in the open, he'd be visible to anyone. He listened. No sounds, other than the birds making their early morning racket.

Sucking in a deep breath, Taylor raced to the flagpole and unwound the halyard rope from its double-pronged cleat. He pulled the shorts from his pocket, attaching one snap hook to the side waistband and the other to the hem of the opposite leg. Any kind of breeze should make the Corvette print stand out. Then, raising the makeshift flag hand-over-hand to the top, he secured the halyard again and ran for the nearby bushes. Another scan for anyone who might be watching and Taylor beat a path straight back to the cabin, stopping outside the door to catch his breath.

He didn't dare open the door until his breathing slowed, but at last he squeezed through and rested the door silently against the jam. He listened, making sure the runners hadn't returned. All was quiet. He stepped toward the bunkroom and his wet foot shot out from under him. His hand caught hold of an armchair to break his fall, but his body still hit the floor with a thump.

Taylor clenched his teeth, squelching a few unsavory words while he massaged his hip. Pulling his legs in close, he rubbed the moisture from the soles of his feet before standing up.

A voice from the bunkroom made him freeze. He waited, listening, but heard nothing more. Padding carefully back to his bunk, he'd almost made it when Steven mumbled, "Oh, good. You're back."

Taylor halted. Just his luck to be caught by the kid who can't see. He whispered to Steven. "Had to use the toilet."

No response. Steven rolled onto his side and snuggled into his sleeping bag, his eyes closed the whole time. *Talking in his sleep?*

Taylor crossed his fingers and slid into his bunk. His sore toe didn't hurt nearly as much as last night, but his cold feet sought the warmth of the sleeping bag and he burrowed into its comfort.

Moments later, the squeak of the screen door signaled the runners' return. Taylor turned to his side, closed his eyes and hid a smile in his pillow. Mission accomplished.

7

T aylor did his best to avoid looking at the flagpole on the way to breakfast. Better to let someone else discover it. He couldn't pass up the chance to see Luke's reaction, so he joined his group heading to breakfast. Luke gave him a curious look.

What if no one noticed the flagpole? Most of the guys looked half asleep as they followed in Harris's footsteps, heads down. Taylor ducked his head and snuck a glance at the flagpole through his hair.

An American flag? What happened to Luke's shorts?

Of course. Zeke always put the flag up before breakfast. He must've take down the boxers when he raised the real flag. All that work for nothing, not to mention losing an hour of sleep.

Taylor moved through the buffet line, loading his plate with scrambled eggs and bacon. He grabbed a slice of toast and some jelly, and joined Nick at a table with Brady and Steven. He set his tray on the table then listened as Zeke made an announcement over the loudspeakers at the back of the room.

"Apparently, our cabins need more storage units for clothes. I'm sorry someone had to resort to using the flagpole instead." He paused as he held up Luke's shorts. "I apologize for any embarrassment this causes, but the owner of these may claim them in my office any time today." He'd barely finished his sentence when the room erupted in whistles and laughter.

This was even better! Luke bragged about his dad's Corvette so much that everyone would guess those were his shorts.

"There he goes." Nick laughed and pointed. Amid the catcalls and laughter, Luke stalked out of the dining hall, leaving his tray of uneaten food on the table. "I guess he doesn't like that kind of attention."

Brady explained the joke to Steven. "I wonder if he'll actually claim them."

Steven chuckled. "Poor guy. Who do you think put them up there?"

Taylor made no comment, and focused on eating his breakfast. He kept an eye out for Marissa, but didn't see her until morning Bible study, and then he was too far away to talk to her. He finally cornered her after lunch. "Where did you and Luke go after chapel last night?"

Rissa frowned at him and set her tray on the conveyor belt for dirty plates and utensils. "Nowhere. What do you care?"

"Your boyfriend didn't get back to the cabin until nearly lights out. Said he was hanging with a friend."

"So?" Marissa tried to leave, but Taylor blocked her way.

"So where were you? What were you doing out after curfew?"

Marissa huffed and planted her hands on her hips. "I was not out after curfew."

"Yeah, right."

"I wasn't. Ask anyone in my cabin. Ask Claire if you don't believe me." Marissa looked him square in the eye.

Maybe she was telling the truth.

"Then who was Luke out with?"

"How should I know?" She threw her hands out, palms up.

"Why don't you ask him? And leave me alone." Marissa pushed him aside and marched out of the dining hall.

Taylor called after her. "Leave him alone, Riss. He's a jerk."

Marissa waved her hand behind her, as if brushing off his advice. At least she wasn't out after curfew last night. Maybe he was worrying over nothing? No. It was only a matter of time before her thirst for adventure kicked in. He'd better be ready for it.

Taylor headed for the Snack Shack to see what his rec team was doing. He looked down the list and found his team. Volleyball. A chick game. Why couldn't they play guys' games, like basketball or football? Turning away from the board, he noticed Roberto and the God Squad guy at the bell tower. The camp pickup was parked on the grass nearby and the two men stood on ladders, one on each side of the tower. The new bell rested atop the platform. Taylor hurried over for a closer look.

Roberto greeted him with a friendly nod as he threaded a rope around the bell's flywheel.

"Are you going to ring it now?" Taylor asked.

"Soon." Roberto asked Paul to make sure the rope was seated correctly behind the wheel. When he finished winding it around again, he looked it all over one last time—clapper, supports, yoke, wheel. He tugged on the rope and watched the wheel turn the bell, catching the clapper before it could make a sound. With a nod to Paul, he pulled out his phone and punched a number. Paul climbed down and stowed his ladder in the back of the pickup.

Roberto spoke into his phone. "Is ready. You come?" He listened for a reply then clicked off. After climbing down his ladder, he laid it in the pickup beside Paul's. He lifted his hat and used his sleeve to wipe the sweat from his forehead, then replaced the hat. "Zeke is coming. He will ring it."

A moment later, Zeke appeared. "No more excuses for missing breakfast, Taylor. This bell will make sure you're awake."

He checked his watch. "Just in time for Rec." Zeke took hold of the rope and pulled down.

The wheel rotated, the yoke turned, the bell tipped.

Clang!

It was a rich, meaty sound. Zeke let up on the rope then pulled again.

Clang! Clang, clang!

Zeke let the clanging diminish then wound the rope around a cleat. Roberto put his tools in the truck and climbed into the driver's seat. Before he started the engine, he called to Taylor. "Tonight?"

Taylor held his thumbs up. "Si! Tonight."

"What's tonight?" Zeke asked.

"He works on the car with me. Good mechanic."

"In the shop? Working on your car?" Zeke looked back and forth between them. "When?"

Zeke's tone didn't sound good. Taylor let Roberto answer.

"After supper. Before evening worship."

Zeke scratched behind his ear, then smoothed his white mustache. "I'm not sure that's such a good idea."

Taylor's shoulders dropped, even as Zeke laid his hands on them.

"You go on to Rec and let me talk with Roberto about this."

Taylor shot a pleading look at Roberto, but the older man dismissed him, pointing his chin in the direction of the Rec field. A wink and one hand raised in a gesture that said *Let me handle this* did little to reassure him.

Sucking in a deep breath, he turned and dragged his feet toward the Rec field. What if Roberto's car turned out like his driver's license—so close, but off limits? He wouldn't be able to stand it. And now he had to play this dumb chick game.

Taylor ignored his teammates, kicking off his flip-flops beside the timbers surrounding the new sand court. He staked out a position on the front row, wiggling his toes into the loose sand, digging his heels deep to where the sand felt cool. Too bad it couldn't chill his mood as well.

Other kids crowded onto both sides of the court until the counselor had to pull some out to rotate in, making sure both sides had an equal number of players. She blew her whistle to start the game and the other team served the ball. It sailed across the net toward Taylor. He jumped and smacked it back. At least he could take out his anger on the ball. Landing in the sand was easy on his sore toe, too.

The score seesawed with the ball dropping out of bounds or hitting the net. When forced to rotate out, Taylor paced the sideline. Even in a stupid game, he'd rather play than watch. By the time he rotated back in, his team was behind 10-6. The serve came across the net and was volleyed a couple times before coming straight at him in the back row. He could really pound it this time. He raised his hands and slammed the ball forward.

The ball shot straight into the net, missing Claire's head by inches. She glared at him from the front line. "Quit trying to show off."

Taylor spread his hands out. "Yeah? Let's see you get it across the net from back here."

"Try setting it up. That's why we're here." She pointed to the front row, rolled her eyes and shook her head.

Taylor's insides burned. Hands on hips, he tromped around in a tight circle, kicking at the sand. Can't a guy make a mistake?

By the time he rotated up to the front again, the other team needed only one point to win. The serve flew back to the third row where Claire stood ready. Fists together, wrists up, she scooped the ball into the air and called for help as it neared the net.

"I got it!" Taylor jumped and spiked the ball to the other side of the net. *Whump!* It hit the ground, and his teammates cheered.

Even Claire gave him a grudging, "Nice shot."

Not much, but he'd take it. Taylor smoothed the sand with his foot. Is that what it took to get her approval?

They lost the game after two more plays and switched sides to start again. Whenever the ball came his way, Taylor tried to set it up for Claire. But the thing usually bounced off his wrists in a random direction. The few times it did find her she popped it over the net. The second game ended in a loss as well, but only by a difference of three points.

Last game. With the score tied at 14-14, Claire moved into server's position. "Come on, you guys! We can win this one. Let's do it!"

She stepped to the corner of the court, tossed the ball in the air and batted it across the net. It volleyed back and forth several times before falling to the ground on the other side. While the other team argued over who should've covered it, Claire hurried into her position on the serving line. "One more and it's ours! Let's take it."

She sent the ball over the net, but the other team sent it right back to her. She popped it into the air. "Taylor, it's yours!"

Taylor eyed the ball as it dropped, timing his jump. At the last second, he leaped into the air and smashed the ball down the other side of the net.

"Game!" called the counselor. Cheers erupted from the team, and his teammates clapped Taylor on the back. Claire ran toward him, both hands in the air for a double high five. A warm glow spread through his chest.

"Nice play!" Her dimpled cheeks glistened and were tinged with pink. Sand smudged her chin on one side.

"Thanks."

Was that all he could say? *Lame.* Claire dropped his hands and shuffled her feet through the sand to the edge of the court. Balancing on a perimeter log, she turned back to Taylor.

"Your sister's crazy. In a cool way, I mean. Crazy cool. I like her." With that, Claire hopped onto the ground and grabbed her sandals. "Wish my little brother bragged about me the way Marissa brags about you."

She exhaled a single laugh, shook her head and hurried to join the other girls on their way to the cabins. Not exactly a compliment, but she hadn't curled her lip or rolled her eyes at him since the first game. Taylor slipped his feet into his flip-flops. Progress, that's what he'd call it. Definitely progress.

8
_____

B ack at the cabin, a couple boys on the other side of the
bunkroom bragged about their rec team's win. Nick sank
onto the bed to wait as Taylor headed for the bathroom
with his swim trunks.

Luke emerged from the bathroom in swim gear, a beach towel
slung around his neck. He blocked Taylor's path. "You. Stay outa
my stuff."

Taylor stuck his chest out. "I don't know what you're talking
about." He held his ground as Luke stepped closer, breathing into
Taylor's face.

"Who else would put my shorts up the flagpole? Keep your
hands off my stuff, y'hear?"

Taylor's pulse accelerated. Could he take Luke in a fight?
Doubtful. The guy was bigger, and he had some muscle. He
jabbed a finger into Luke's chest. "I didn't touch your stinking
shorts. You stay away from my sister."

Luke grabbed Taylor's t-shirt in his fists and backed him up
against the end of Steven's bunk. "No one tells me what to do,
especially punks like you."

The boys on the other side of the room fell silent. Of course, they'd be watching, but where was Nick? Why didn't he jump in to help? Taylor dropped his swim trunks to the floor and wedged his hands against Luke's chest, trying to put more distance between them, but Luke leaned into him even harder.

Taylor's teeth clenched. "Leave Rissa alone." He lowered his right hand and thrust a fist into Luke's side, only to take a blow to the gut. Air whooshed from his body.

"Fight! Fight!" The boys on the other side of the room chanted.

Nick sprang from Taylor's bed and tugged on Luke's arm. "Let go. Leave him alone."

The door to Harris's room flew open and the counselor filled the bunkroom doorway. "Break it up! Knock it off."

Luke eased the pressure. His lip curled in a sneer as he released his hold on Taylor and yanked his arm from Nick's grasp.

Harris eyed them, nostrils flaring. "Morning runs not enough for you, Luke? That means even earlier tomorrow and we'll add some crunches and pushups as well." He tipped his head to one side and looked at Taylor. "And you get to join us."

Taylor stepped sideways. "Why? I didn't start it! He pushed me "

"Did I ask who started anything?" Harris's dark eyes challenged Taylor to disagree. His right hand played toss-and-catch with a ring of keys. "Both of you can expect an early wake-up call tomorrow. And it'll only get earlier if there's any more fighting." He gave them a humorless smile. "Your choice."

With a huff, Taylor snatched his trunks off the floor, pushed past Luke and escaped into the bathroom. He clamped his mouth shut to keep from spewing the words on the tip of his tongue. Harris was right—it was way tougher to hold them in than to let them gush out. He leaned against the sink, taking deep breaths, willing his heart to slow down.

The screen door squeaked and slammed. Probably Luke leaving. *Too bad it's not for good.*

Nick poked his head into the bathroom. "Are you okay? What was that all about?"

Taylor answered Nick's reflection in the mirror. "He thinks I'm the one who put his shorts up the flagpole this morning."

Nick's mouth went through several contortions. "Um...did you?"

Taylor couldn't admit anything, no matter how tempting it was to share some laughs with his friend. "Doesn't matter if I did or not. He's convinced I did." Taylor slapped his swim shorts against the counter. "I don't feel like swimming anymore."

"Why? Because he's down there?" Nick blew a breath between his lips. "You gonna let him decide what you do? That'd make him real happy."

Nick was right. Taylor changed into his swim shorts and they headed down to the beach. Claire, Brady and Steven were among the kids waiting to use the diving board, but no Luke. Where was he? In the water? Taylor dropped his towel on the sand and waded into the water, scanning the lakefront for Luke.

A canoe was returning to the boat dock, its crew frantically trying to steer around it. The bow bumped against a corner, and the counselor in charge waded in to tow them to shore. Another canoe launched, gliding past the swimming pier and the boundary ropes that marked the deep-water swim area. Marissa paddled in front, Luke in back.

What would Rissa say about Luke picking a fight with him? Would she still be all gooey about him and take his side? Or would she jump to Taylor's defense, the way they'd done for each other ever since he could remember? For once, he had no clue.

TUESDAY NIGHT'S picnic supper did little to stir Taylor's appetite.

He waited while Janie placed a fresh pan of sloppy joe sandwiches on the outdoor serving table. Normally, he'd grab two or three, but nothing looked good after finding out Zeke wouldn't let him work on the car. Roberto had been in the cabin fixing a clogged toilet when Taylor returned from swimming. He gave Taylor the bad news.

The aroma of barbecue filled his nostrils as Janie pulled back the foil from the tray of hot sandwiches. "There you go. Help yourself." She took a second look at Taylor. "Aren't you the young man who's helping my husband work on his car?"

"I was." Taylor shook the hair back from his eyes.

Janie clapped her hands together. "He is so excited to have someone share his love of cars. Neither of our boys showed any interest."

Roberto must not have told her about Zeke, maybe because he still believed he could change Zeke's mind.

Janie peered at Taylor across the table. "You do like working on cars, don't you?"

"Yeah, I love cars. But Zeke found out and now he won't let me do it anymore."

Janie straightened. "What?" She scowled, wringing a white dishtowel in her hands. "Zeke said no?"

"Rober—Mr. Rodriguez thinks he can persuade Zeke to change his mind, but " Taylor shrugged.

Janie slapped the towel over her shoulder. "Well, if he doesn't, I will. I've never seen the man so happy as when he told me how you admired his car. He looked like a little boy on Christmas morning." She shook a finger at Taylor. "Don't you worry. You'll be back in that garage soon. Now, eat up!" She encouraged him to take more sandwiches, but Taylor moved on to dessert.

Zeke's decision meant Taylor would have to play the dumb after-supper game. Would anyone notice if he hid out in the woods for a while?

Before anyone wandered away after supper, Zeke climbed

onto the bed of the pickup truck and raised a bullhorn to his mouth. "For tonight's game, you're competing against the other seven cabins, so you'll need to find your cabin mates and stick together in a group."

There went his chance to hide in the woods. Someone would miss him for sure. Worse, he'd be spending the next hour with Luke as well. *Barf.*

Brady and Steven came up beside Taylor. Brady jerked his head toward Steven. "Can he hang out with you? He's in your cabin, right?"

"Yeah, sure." Taylor shouldered up next to Steven as Brady left to find his cabin group. "Actually, I was thinking about hiding out in the woods until the game's over. Or are you into these things?"

Steven lifted his foot and wiggled his toes. "Not unless I go back and put shoes on. Last year, Brady and I got poison ivy walking through the woods."

"Oh. Probably not a good idea then." At least, Luke wouldn't harass him much with Steven close by.

Minutes later, Taylor and Steven joined their cabin group, and Zeke finished his instructions. "Tonight, you're on a counselor hunt. All eight counselors are hiding in various places around the camp. They'll be outside and in plain view, but not necessarily easily seen or recognized." He held up a stack of papers and a fistful of pens. "Each cabin group needs a pen and one of these sheets that lists the counselors' names with a place for their signature. When you find a counselor, they must sign their name to prove you found them. The first cabin to return here to me with all eight signatures wins an ice cream treat from the Snack Shack. And let me remind you, forgery is a sin. Any team caught forging signatures will pick up trash around camp during the first hour of afternoon free time tomorrow. Any questions?"

Taylor whispered to Steven. "Doesn't it get old, not being able to do stuff like this?"

"Who says I can't?"

"But you can't see where the counselors are."

Steven laughed. "You forget, I've done this before. I may not be able to see them, but I know where to look. Without me, you guys won't even come close to winning."

Taylor grinned. "You are a genius."

Steven laughed again. "Thanks. Who has the list of names?"

Luke moseyed up to the group as Taylor called everyone in close. "Hey, pay attention! Steven's going to tell us how to win this game."

Steven called out. "Okay, the counselors will be "

"Not so loud," Taylor warned. "There's other groups around."

"Oh. Sorry." Steven lowered his voice. "The counselors are in plain view, but they're disguised. Look for people doing normal things, like taking the trash out from the kitchen, or raking, or working in a flowerbed. Think about it. Most of the staff is off duty by now so anyone still working is probably a counselor. They may be dressed to look like Nurse Willie or Roberto or maybe even Zeke."

Luke pointed. "There's someone in a hat and work gloves." He grabbed the paper and pen and took off. A few of the other boys followed.

"Wait!" Steven turned toward Taylor. "Did he leave already? I thought you said there're other groups around."

"Yeah, and Luke showed them all where to find their first counselor. Everyone's getting that signature. What an idiot."

Luke returned, waving the sheet in triumph. "One down. That was easy."

Taylor scowled. "Yeah, especially for those other two cabins. Next time, wait."

Luke's hands dropped to his sides. The paper flapped against his leg. "Who cares? It's only a stupid game, anyway."

That's one thing they agreed on, though Taylor would never admit it.

Steven held up his hand. "Don't worry about it. But next time, try to make sure no one else is around to see you."

Taylor had an idea. "Maybe only one of us should get the signature. If we act like we're looking for something, the rest of us can spread out, kind of like a screen so other teams can't see who's getting the signature."

The other boys agreed and they wandered around the end of the chapel toward the lake. A different group had fanned out along the waterfront. Taylor glanced back at the chapel and noticed a figure hunched over the side garden. He hissed at Luke for the signature sheet.

Luke frowned and held the paper against his chest. "I'll get the signature."

Taylor huffed, but Luke was already on his way. He whistled softly to the other boys, motioning them to close in a bit without making it obvious.

Luke returned with another scribble on the page. "There. Satisfied?" He thrust the paper and pen into Steven's hand and cut Taylor's reply short. "Actually, you can do it yourself next time."

He broke away and went galloping down the hill toward the group of girls searching the waterfront. Marissa separated from the group and met him with a huge smile.

Taylor's stomach churned. He would've turned around and searched somewhere else, but the rest of the guys followed Luke's lead. He and Steven tromped down the hill.

Claire waved to them as they approached. "How many have you found?"

Steven hid the paper behind his back. "None of your business, but I bet it's more than you."

Claire laughed. "No way. You're not the only one who's done this before. We're going to win this one."

"Oh yeah? Guess you'll have to prove it." Steven tugged on Taylor's arm. "C'mon, let's get moving or we'll run out of time." He whispered to Taylor. "Try the boat dock."

Taylor called the others to follow, and took a wandering path toward the boat dock. Luke hung back, catching up to the group as they neared the steps leading down to the dock. The boathouse door was closed and padlocked, the motorboat sat high on its lift and six canoes lined the bank, bottoms up.

"I don't see anyone." Taylor turned away, but Steven held him back.

"Check everywhere. There's always been someone hiding here."

The boys spread out and soon a shout came from the opposite side of the boathouse. "Hey, over here!"

Taylor winced. Nothing like announcing it to the whole camp. He and Steven hurried around to the other side. Brush lined the sides of two parallel ruts sloping down to the lake. A lone figure stood painting the wood-frame gate across the boat launch entrance. Taylor recognized Roberto's hat, but the brown uniform shirt and pants fit too well for it to be Roberto.

Luke laughed. "That's Harris."

Taylor checked to be certain no other groups were within eyesight before bringing Steven close to get Harris's signature.

The counselor kept his head bowed so the hat hid his face, and signed his name without a word. A sudden shriek brought his head up with a jerk.

"Snake! A snake crawled over my foot."

The soles of Luke's bare feet kicked up grass as he fled. When he finally stopped some distance away, he kept hopping, lifting his feet high in the air as if trying to avoid touching the ground.

"Kill it! Someone get it!" Luke's arms flailed.

Harris studied the ground then grabbed at something.

It took a few tries before he held up a slender, wriggling gray snake with a white stripe down the length of its back. "Is this what you're scared of? I've seen earthworms bigger than this."

"I hate snakes." Luke's voice cracked and he turned away, hurrying off in the direction of the cabin. Harris called after him, but Luke kept going.

Taylor laughed, his guffaws joining Harris and the others. Who would've guessed Corvette Boy was terrified of snakes?

Perfect. This was perfect.

9

*L*uke's afraid of snakes. Not just afraid, but terrified.

Taylor's mind churned with possibilities, oblivious to the kids around him clapping and swaying with the beat of the evening worship music. He grinned at the memory of Luke's shriek and the way he hopped from one foot to the other. Priceless.

Nick tugged on the leg of his shorts. "Hey, dude, you can sit down any time."

The music had finished and everyone else was sitting. Taylor sank onto the seat as Zeke moved to the stage and set up his easel. With Luke on his mind, it'd be nearly impossible to pay attention. But in case Roberto ever asked, he needed to know at least something of what Zeke talked about tonight.

Zeke turned his pad of paper sideways and made two black circles. "I have four brothers, one younger than me by about four years. With three older brothers, I got a lot of hand-me-downs. Clothes, shoes, toys, bikes. We did a lot of bike riding, and you can imagine what kind of shape the bike was in by the time my older brothers had outgrown it."

He drew some red lines to connect the black circles into the outline of a bicycle. "One day, I saw a shiny new bike in a store window downtown. It was fire engine red with gleaming chrome handlebars. It had a banana seat. Those were all the rage at the time. More than once, I asked my parents to buy the bike for me. Their answer was always, 'We'll see.'"

Zeke turned and faced the campers. "Do your parents ever say that? 'We'll see.' It took me years to figure out it was a polite way of saying no. The way I remember it, I begged my parents for that bike every time we passed the store. One time, my little brother was with us when I asked for the bike and he said he wanted a bike, too.

"Well, months later, his birthday came around and guess what my parents gave him. Not just any bike. My bike. The one I'd begged for. The bike I'd dreamed of riding. It wasn't fair. A seed of envy sprouted that day, and I watered it well. Every time I saw him riding 'my' bike, I grew more and more jealous of him, until one day I decided to teach my little brother a lesson."

Zeke finished the drawing, put his chalk away and faced the campers. He dug his hands into his pants pockets.

"One November day, I took his bike and hid it. Buried it under a pile of brush and leaves my dad had raked up. When my brother asked if I'd seen it, I said no and scolded him for not putting it away the last time he rode it. He said he had put it away, but I pretended I didn't believe him." Zeke bowed his head, scuffed his shoe against the floor.

The room fell silent. Taylor guessed what happened. He could see it coming when Zeke raised his head.

"That weekend, my dad burned the leaf pile. I'd never smelled burning rubber before. And to this day, that awful, acrid odor reminds me of how destructive jealousy can be. My jealousy hurt my brother far more than I'd intended. It destroyed a beautiful bicycle. I destroyed the very bicycle I'd wanted so badly." Zeke walked the aisle, stopping now and then, hands still deep in his pockets. "My parents never pressured us to confess how the bike got there, though I'm guessing they had a pretty strong suspicion. They simply left that horrible, charred bike out where I could see it. Every day. Every time I walked out the door, I got a vivid reminder of what jealousy is capable of doing."

Zeke reached the back of the room beside where Taylor was sitting.

"The Bible is full of stories about anger and jealousy. Right from the beginning, Cain's anger and jealousy prompted him to murder his brother Abel. Joseph's jealous brothers sold him into slavery. Daniel was thrown to hungry lions because the other overseers were jealous of his reputation and abilities. Jesus' own disciples struggled with jealousy among themselves. And jealous Jewish leaders crucified God's own son."

On a slow pace back up the aisle, Zeke asked his question of the week. "What's in your heart? Gossip, lies and insults? Pride and arrogance? Anger and jealousy? In the Sermon on the Mount, Jesus equated anger with murder. The Bible also lists jealousy among the traits of God's enemies. James says that where you have envy, you find disorder and all kinds of evil deeds. Peter tells us to put it aside, get rid of it."

Zeke stopped at the front, near the stage, and gazed out at the campers in the chapel. "What's in your heart?"

Marissa passed Taylor on her way out of the chapel, wiggling her fingers in the secret wave they used at school to avoid notice by the teachers. Taylor didn't return the signal, not with Luke right behind her. Seeing them together nauseated him.

Luke bent to whisper something in Marissa's ear, and she responded with wide eyes and a mischievous grin.

Uh, oh. He'd seen that look before. His life was about to get complicated real fast. Taylor followed them out the door, watching until they separated with a *See you later* and Luke headed to the cabin. *Later?* Meaning tomorrow? Or tonight?

Taylor kept an eye on Luke in the cabin. Would Luke try to sneak out tonight, maybe after everyone was asleep? If he did, Taylor would have to follow him to find Marissa and make her return to her cabin.

Luke was still in his shorts during cabin devotions, but then so were a couple other guys. His eyes often fixed on the door. Was he scheming how to get out without the squeak giving him away? Harris finally dismissed them, and Taylor stood up, stretched and yawned as if he couldn't wait to get to sleep.

"Remember," Harris said, "you and Luke and I have an early appointment tomorrow morning."

Taylor groaned and slumped. He'd forgotten all about their early morning workout. Maybe Luke wouldn't sneak out tonight after all. But he still needed to stay awake long enough to find out. And that made tomorrow morning a problem.

The moment Luke's foot cleared the windowsill, Taylor slipped out of bed and hurried to see which way he went. The light in Harris's bedroom had been off for at least an hour. Deep breathing and soft snores filled the bunkroom as Taylor peeked out the window, careful not to disturb the screen Luke had set on the floor. The moonlight caught Luke's bare back as he jogged between trees past the chapel.

Taylor picked up the screen and set it on Luke's bed, then followed him out the window and past the chapel. The nearly full moon illuminated the ground, casting shadows from the trees, and Taylor stayed in the dark shadows as much as possible. No sense giving himself away until he knew Marissa was out here, too. But where was Luke? He'd lost him in the time it took to climb out the window. *Think.* Where would you go if you wanted to meet up with someone, especially a girl?

Taylor moved toward the girls' cabins. He peeked around a tree trunk, but the only motion near Marissa's cabin was the on and off glow of fireflies. Where else could she and Luke have gone? The woods? Marissa wouldn't go near the woods in the dark. Besides, the mosquitoes would eat them alive.

A giggle, quickly stifled, sounded to his right. The lake! Stooping low and moving from shadow to shadow, Taylor made his way toward the beach. The floodlights that usually lit the lakefront at night were dark, probably set to go off at midnight. The gate to the beach would be locked, but with so much open lakeshore, anyone could step into the water and wade over to the swimming area as long as they didn't mind stepping on rocks instead of sand. Taylor caught a glimpse of Luke and Marissa as they hurried across a moonlit spot. Hand in hand, they moved along the edge where the ground made a steep drop to the lake.

Taylor ran the other way, toward the boat dock. Strange that the swimming area had a locked gate but nothing blocked entry to the boat dock. Except for that flimsy one across the boat launch—a square frame with a couple crosspieces, secured by a fork latch. He hurried down to the lake. It was warm as bath water as Taylor eased in, crouching and moving out until he was neck deep. Silently, he worked his way around the boat dock and over to the swimming pier. The night air carried Luke's and Marissa's whispers across the water, but he couldn't make out their words. Only an occasional soft sploosh as they dipped in and out. Their silhouettes rose from the surface within the area bounded by the swimming pier. Marissa's shoulders shone white in the bright glow of the moon.

Taylor stopped outside the pier, near enough now to hear Luke warn Marissa about staying low in the water to avoid detection. Taylor ran his hands along the pier's supports until he found an open spot, then slipped into the sheer darkness underwater and pulled himself between the supports. He resurfaced within the shallow swimming area and without thinking, whipped his head back to shake the hair from his eyes. Droplets of water pelted the surface.

Marissa gasped. "What was that?" Their two shadows froze in the moonlight. Luke spoke just above a whisper. "Who's there?"

No use hiding anymore. Taylor stood up.

"It's me."

"Taylor?" Marissa's voice squeaked.

Even in the dark, Luke's sneer was obvious. "What are you doing here?"

"Trying to keep my sister out of trouble." Taylor moved closer, but kept some distance between them, in case Luke threatened him again.

"She's not in trouble so you can get lost."

Marissa slapped her hands on the water. "I can't believe you followed us down here." A dog barked from a neighboring yard, and she cut her voice to a whisper again. "You don't have to stand guard over me, Taybo. I'm a big girl now."

"Then prove it and get back to your cabin before you get caught."

Luke moved toward him. "We won't get caught. No one knows we're here."

Marissa dunked her head, letting the water pull her hair back from her face. "We won't be here long. We only wanted to see what it was like to swim in the dark. Go back to your cabin and leave us alone."

Taylor stood his ground. "I'm not leaving until you go back to your cabin."

A light flared from the hill above the beach, catching Taylor in its beam. He whirled away from its blinding glare, hissing at Luke. "Get her out of here. Now! Don't let them catch her."

Luke and Marissa dove under the pier and splashed back to where they entered the water. Covering for them, Taylor splashed as much as he could while plunging in the opposite direction. With luck, that flashlight would stay focused on him. He had to give Luke a chance to get Marissa back to her cabin without getting caught. Taylor turned and dove under water, surfacing under the pier.

Whoever held the flashlight moved the beam quickly over the rest of the swimming area. Taylor splashed to draw it back to him.

"Come on out," a voice from the flashlight ordered. "And bring your friends with you."

Paul, the guy from the God Squad. Taylor ducked underwater again and swam halfway back to the boat dock, making sure to splash a few times. A couple trees and lots of weeds and bushes crowded the shoreline between the beach and the boat dock. Taylor crawled onto shore and hid behind the largest tree.

"You want to play hide and seek?" Paul's light splashed across the tree that hid Taylor. "Just warning you, I've never lost a game yet."

Could he stay quiet and hidden long enough to evade capture? Doubtful, but he had to try. The longer he played this out, the better chance Marissa had of returning to her cabin.

The light bounced around, moving closer. Paul spoke to someone, but Taylor heard no response. Was he on his phone?

Taylor peered out at the lake. Should he climb the tree or go back into the water to hide? If he went back in, he couldn't stay under forever, and every time he surfaced, the ripples would give him away. The moon was so bright he could see the undulations of the water around the boat dock. But when he looked up, the lowest tree branch was just beyond his reach. He'd have to jump, and there'd be no second chance. If he missed, the rustle of his landing would give away his exact location.

Crouching, Taylor gazed up into the tree and planned his jump. Moonlight outlined the branch and he closed his eyes, imagining the distance, the thickness of the branch. He flexed on his knees twice, just like on the diving board, then launched himself upward. His hands caught the branch while his body swung back and forth. For once, he was sorry he hadn't worked harder in P.E. A few more pull-ups might've helped right about now. He walked his feet up the trunk far enough to hook one leg over the branch.

The light bobbed closer and the rustling grew louder as he pulled himself up onto the branch. His breathing alone could give him away. Taylor opened his mouth and forced himself to breathe slow and even. He needed to climb higher but his pursuer was too close. Weeds and brush rustled as Paul pushed his way through, stopping just to the left of Taylor's hiding spot.

A mosquito feasted on Taylor's cheek, but he didn't dare move. He held his breath as the flashlight's beam shone on the water, crossing paths with the moon's reflection. Paul ambled over and squatted beside Taylor's tree. He flicked off the light.

A lone motorboat puttered across the lake. When the noise died away, Paul spoke.

"You want to come down now or wait a little? I got all night. It's up to you."

10

T aylor collapsed onto his bed after the early morning torture session. His whole body ached, worse than any gym class ever. Harris was not a happy camper last night when Paul woke him up, and this morning he made Taylor pay for it. Along with running as punishment for his fight with Luke, Harris made him do push-ups and crunches and more push-ups and more crunches. Now his arms flopped like spaghetti noodles, his gut insisted someone had used it for a punching bag.

All during the workout, Luke wore that irritating smirk. The jerk had made it back to the cabin and pretended to be sound asleep through the whole confrontation in Harris's room last night. Taylor was one breath away from ratting out Luke, but that meant getting Marissa in trouble, too. If he wanted his driver's license, he couldn't let that happen.

Taylor groaned and pulled the sleeping bag over his head to shut out the noise from the other boys getting up and off to breakfast. His stomach hurt so badly, he might skip breakfast and sleep for another hour.

Not a chance. Harris prodded him out of bed.

"Up and at 'em, Taylor. Breakfast. You also have an appointment with Zeke this morning."

Harris made sure he got out of bed, out the door and to the dining hall where Zeke was waiting for him.

"Let's go to my office."

So much for staying out of trouble. He might as well kiss that drivers' license good-bye forever. He'd be an old man before he got his license if Dad found out about this.

Zeke led him down a wide hallway to his office and closed the door behind them. He motioned Taylor into one of two armchairs in front of his desk. Large windows occupied most of the two outer walls. One commanded a nice a view of the lake. Zeke half-sat on his desk in front of Taylor, crossed his arms and tipped his head to look at him. "I hear you went for a midnight swim last night. All by yourself?"

Taylor shoved his hands into his armpits and nodded, forcing himself to meet Zeke's gaze.

"Seems odd to go swimming in the dark by yourself. Can you tell me what prompted such an idea?"

Taylor shrugged one shoulder. "Just felt like swimming."

"Do you understand how dangerous that was, not only swimming alone, but in the dark? What if you'd slipped and hit your head on the pier? I know you weren't planning on that happening, but there's a reason we call them accidents. We don't expect them to happen."

Zeke studied him until Taylor felt like a bug under a microscope. He gazed at his knees, the floor then out the window. Finally, Zeke moved around behind his desk and sank into his chair. He rested his elbows on the desk, chin on his clasped hands as if deep in prayer. A moment later, he opened his Bible, pulled a blank index card out of his desk and slid them both across the desk toward Taylor.

"Read Matthew 7, verse 26."

Taylor scooted the chair up close to the desk and ran his finger over the page until he found the verse.

"But everyone who hears these words of mine and does not put them into practice is like a foolish man who built his house on sand." He glanced up at Zeke, who handed him a pen.

"Write it out on the card, and say it out loud as you write it."

Taylor said the words, pausing between each one to scribble them onto the index card. He laid the pen down on the desk. Zeke closed the Bible.

"Now, read it back to me one more time." Taylor squinted at his writing and repeated the verse. "Do you know that story, Taylor? What happened to the house built on the sand?"

"It collapsed."

"That's right." Zeke leaned forward. "Outside forces damaged the house. Our rules here at camp are meant to keep you safe, so you don't end up like that house on the sand. Ignoring them could very well result in danger and serious injury. Does that make sense?"

Taylor's mouth pulled to one side. "Yeah."

I get it, but the whole thing was never my idea. Marissa needs to hear this more than I do.

Zeke rose to his feet. "Take that card with you and read it during the day. You know the drill. Any time we meet, I want to hear you say the verse out loud." He came around the desk and laid a hand on Taylor's shoulder. "If I know Harris, he's already disciplined you enough to make you think twice about swimming at night. And that means you're pretty hungry by now, so go get something to eat before Janie closes up shop."

Taylor hustled out the door but Zeke called him back. The director smoothed his white mustache with his thumb and forefinger. "Janie tells me Roberto needs you to help him work on his car. I disagree, but I'll give my permission under one condition." He crossed his arms and fixed Taylor with a piercing look. "I don't want to see you in my office again. Understood?"

Taylor's lips spread into a wide smile. "Yes, sir! I understand perfectly. Thanks!" He hurried to the dining hall and lingered through the buffet line, hoping to see Janie to thank her. But he saw only the girls who worked in the kitchen replenishing the food. Maybe he'd catch her at lunch.

Marissa swooped by his table and set her tray with dirty dishes down next to his.

"Thanks for covering for us last night. I almost didn't make it to the cabin." Her voice was just loud enough for him to hear over the din of the dining hall.

"What happened? You guys almost get caught?"

Marissa pulled out the chair next to him and sat down on the edge of it.

"I don't know. There was a second guy out hunting us, but I think when Luke took off for his cabin, the guy followed him. I was so scared. I've never run so fast in my whole life." A sly smile stole across her mouth and her eyes sparkled. "That was so much fun."

"Yeah, fun for you, but I got caught." He gulped his orange juice, the sweetness mixing well with the salty bacon.

Marissa gasped. "Oh Taybo! What happened?"

"The guy knew exactly where I was hiding. He took me back to the cabin, woke up Harris, who was not happy. Harris made me get up at dawn to run with him and that jerk boyfriend of yours "

"He is not a jerk. You'd like him if you'd give him a chance."

"Rissa, he left you alone to save his own skin. He's cocky, thinks he's better than everyone else."

Rissa stood up. "No, he's not. You're just jealous because you got caught and we didn't."

Taylor frowned at his sister. "I'm the reason you didn't get caught. And don't you dare do something stupid again. I'm tired of paying for your little adventures."

"No one asked you to join us last night." Her hands flew to her hips. "You're the one who decided to crash the party, so don't complain to me about getting caught."

Taylor pushed back his chair and stood nose to nose with her. "Okay. I won't crash anymore of your little parties. Let's see how long it takes you to figure out that your idea of fun means trouble." He snatched his tray and stalked over to set it on the conveyor belt.

Marissa grabbed hers and followed him.

"Fine. I don't need you anyway, so don't even bother talking to me." She dropped her tray on the belt and brushed past him, her nose in the air.

A sense of relief washed over him, but it didn't last. She'd do something else before the week was over. The tightening knot in his gut told him so.

HUMAN FOOSBALL. A step above volleyball, maybe, but shooting baskets would be much better than trying to kick this ball past three lines of defenders. He caught the soccer ball beneath his foot. The goal, a soccer net, sat below the backboard at the other end of the basketball court. His hands slid along the waist-high rope stretched across the width of the concrete court. He angled for a better shot at the goal, but the opposing team's mid-field line, his own attack line, the defense and goalkeeper lines stood between him and the goal.

Claire glanced at him from the attack line. A slight jerk of her head signaled she was ready. He kicked the ball, a clear shot straight to her. She added a strong kick that sent it racing past the defenders and goalkeepers into the goal.

"No!" The other team moaned and protested, but Taylor's team erupted in cheers as the score tipped in their favor.

"Come on, we can win this," Claire called. "Let's do it!"

Only two more points. But the other team managed to even

the score and pull ahead, and Dillon's shot-assist from Brady won the game.

Claire came up to Taylor, her hands in the air for a double high five.

"Good game," she said. "That was a nice shot at the end."

Taylor slapped her hands. "You're the one who drove it into the goal."

"Just lucky." She shrugged and left to join Brady and Dillon. Taylor almost called her back to ask if she'd heard Marissa come in last night after her little escapade. But what did it matter? He wasn't responsible for his sister anymore. Let her figure her own way out of trouble.

Taylor headed back to the cabins to find Nick. He passed the bell tower with the camp's pickup parked next to it. Roberto knelt on the ground as Taylor approached.

"Is something wrong?"

Roberto pushed back his hat with a dirt-covered gloved hand. "No. I put in a flower bed." He gestured at the mound of dirt that circled the tower. A path of four round stepping–stones in front of the tower allowed access to the bell. Flats of red, white and purple petunias sat on the pickup's tailgate.

Roberto set one of the flats on the ground and dug his trowel into the dirt, creating a hole. He pulled a flower from the flat, dropped it into the hole, then moved a few inches and repeated the motion. This time, his digging unearthed a fat wriggling worm that he held up for Taylor's inspection.

"You like to fish?"

Taylor shook his head. "No, but Nurse Willie would like that."

Roberto chuckled. "Si, si." He dropped it back into the dirt along with another flower. "So, I see you tonight? We work on car?"

"Yeah! I can't wait." He paused, then said, "Zeke said Janie talked him into letting me work on your car. Is that right?"

Roberto nodded. "Si. Who can stand when Juanie shakes her

finger?" He pointed his index finger and imitated the shaking, then laughed and spread his hands out. "No one argues with Juanie. Not me. Not even Zeke."

Taylor laughed, imagining Zeke caving in to his cook. "I'll be sure to thank her. See you tonight." He hurried back to the cabin to find Nick waiting for him. Within five minutes, they headed for the beach. The afternoon sun was getting hot and that water would feel great.

Taylor kicked his flip-flops off on the sand, dropped his towel and raced Nick into the water. As soon as he was knee deep, he dove under, then surfaced and threw a challenge to Nick.

"Last one to the raft pays for ice cream."

"You're on."

The lifeguard standing on the pier would surely catch him if he tried to swim under it so Taylor hoisted himself up from the shallow end and over into the deep side. His arms and legs churned the water, but Nick stuck right beside him. He sucked in a breath and got a mouthful of turbulent water, spit it out and tried again, this time facing away from Nick. It carried him the rest of the way and he slapped the side of the raft, only to find Nick there at the same time. The two of them gulped air, trying to catch their breath.

"Tie," Nick declared as he exhaled.

Taylor nodded and pulled himself up the ladder. Nick followed. Minutes later, Luke climbed onto the raft. He jacked up his trunks with a smug grin, as if expecting them to applaud his presence. Taylor ignored him, until Luke sidled up next to him and spoke in a low voice.

"Nice of you to cover for us last night."

Taylor regarded him through narrowed eyes. "I was covering for Marissa, not you. You could've stuck around to make sure she got back to her cabin without getting caught."

"She didn't get caught, did she?"

"No thanks to you. Just don't try anything like that again. I'm not bailing out either one of you next time." Taylor pushed past Luke, making sure to bump his shoulder in the process, and stepped up on the diving board. He took a running leap and dove into the water.

Nick was waiting for him in the water after Taylor surfaced. "What'd you say to Luke?"

Taylor swam away from the diving area before answering. "He and Rissa snuck out and met down here to swim after lights out last night. I followed him. And I'm the one who got caught."

"You? What about him and your sister?"

Taylor explained what had happened, then suggested they go get some ice cream.

Nick side-stroked to the pier. "I heard he freaked out over a little grass snake last night. Is that true?"

Taylor laughed out loud. "That was so funny. I wish Rissa'd seen her hero running scared, squealing like a pig." He laughed again, and an image of Roberto holding up that wriggling earthworm came to mind. Snakes worms hmmm.

Time to visit Nurse Willie.

11

N urse Willie clicked off the penlight and let go of Taylor's eyelid. "I don't see anything that shouldn't be there. Maybe some drops will help soothe the irritation. Probably just an allergy to the grass or trees or something around here."

Taylor blinked his eye a few times, then tipped his head back while Willie squirted some drops.

"If it doesn't clear up by tomorrow, come back and let me take another look at it."

Taylor dabbed his eye with a tissue while Nurse Willie washed her hands and put away her penlight and the eye drops. He coughed and cleared his throat. "Um, can I ask you...what kind of bait do you use for fishing?"

Nurse Willie turned a raised eyebrow his way. "Since when are you interested in fishing?"

"Just wondering." Taylor shrugged. "Thought I might try it while I'm here."

Willie pursed her lips, then opened a small cooler beneath her desk and took out a Styrofoam dish like the ones mashed potatoes came in at the fried chicken restaurants. She peeled off the cover and held the container out for his inspection. A fat worm wiggled down into the dirt. "Nightcrawlers."

Perfect.

"Do you buy them or dig 'em up yourself?"

Willie scowled. "Waste of good money to buy them. You can find them down there by the lake where it's kind of marshy at the edge of the woods. Go at night, especially after a good rain. Take a flashlight and you'll be pulling them out of the ground like weeds." She replaced the cover and set the dish back in the cooler, then reached up and opened the cupboard above her desk. A small stack of Styrofoam dishes sat way up on the top shelf. She handed one to Taylor.

"It's been so dry lately, you might not see many. But fill this with moist dirt before you go looking. Nightcrawlers need to stay moist and cool. Let 'em get too warm and you'll have a stinky, gooey mess. You might ask for a cup of ice at the Shack to keep them cool."

Taylor smiled as he exited the clinic. The something-in- the-eye complaint worked like grease on a hinge. Willie practically gave him her own stash of worms. Now, if he could beat the crowd out of chapel tonight, he'd have ten minutes to nab a couple nightcrawlers and get back to the cabin. No need for ice. He'd have to ditch the cup, too. Wouldn't want anyone to notice him bringing a white cup into the cabin. If he carried the worms in his hands, nobody would know. And if the nightcrawlers turned into a stinky, gooey mess later well, that might be just as much fun.

~

TAYLOR RAN to the machine shed as soon as he finished supper. Roberto was waiting for him.

"Ready to work?" Roberto picked up a piece of new carpet lying on the driveway. It was molded to fit over the hump that ran through the center of the car. The tractor that was normally parked in the bay next to the Mustang sat outside next to the carpet pieces. In its place were the Mustang's front bucket seats and the back seat. The car's dirty old carpet lay in a stiff heap between the bays.

Roberto thrust one end of the carpet into the car through the driver's door to Taylor on the other side. The car had been gutted —seats, carpet, seatbelts. Everything had been removed down to the floor pan. Only the gearshift lever and the steering column remained. Roberto had already added a new floor liner, and Taylor tugged the carpet into place over it.

Roberto measured, made a slit in the carpet and fitted it down around the gearshift lever. "I leave carpet out in sun today, so is warm. Bends easy."

Taylor pressed the carpet down his side of the hump in the middle, up under the dashboard, and out to the passenger door. "Good idea. It's not hard to work with at all." When the carpet lay flat enough to satisfy Roberto, they went to work on the back half.

Clang. Clang. Clang, clang. The bell called campers to evening worship.

Taylor looked up from pressing the back carpet down towards the rear of the car. "Already? I just got here."

Sweat dripping from his nose, Roberto sat back on his heels and shook his head. "I hoped we could put in the seats."

"Do I have to go?" Taylor pressed his advantage as the bell's clanging died off. "Ple-ease?"

Roberto chewed his lip, staring at the carpet. His head bobbed once. "I like you to stay, but you go. Zeke will look for you in chapel, but," he wagged his finger, "tomorrow we put seats in." He stopped and tilted his head, as if listening to an inaudible voice. "My daughter—her baby comes any day now." Roberto put his palms together. "But we will pray she waits until after tomorrow. Okay?"

Taylor frowned and backed out of the car. Roberto came to him, laying an arm across his shoulders.

"You are good worker. You love car like I do."

A smile pulled at one corner of Taylor's mouth. "Yeah, I do. Someday, maybe I'll restore a car like this." He met Roberto's gaze. "Thanks for letting me help."

Roberto laughed and clapped him on the shoulder. "Tomorrow night, we finish the seats."

TAYLOR TOOK his time getting back to the cabin to grab his flashlight before heading to evening worship. The band was already playing when he stepped into the chapel. Purposely late, he checked to make sure Nick hadn't saved him a seat and wasn't watching for him. If he sat alone near the back, he wouldn't have to explain to anyone why he needed to race out the door as soon as the service ended. He'd still have to beat the crowd by jumping into the aisle the moment Zeke said the prayer's amen.

Taylor selected a seat, mentally sketching out his plan while the band played and led worship. By the time Zeke stepped onto the stage, he was itching to go hunt nightcrawlers. How would he ever sit through Zeke's message now? Maybe he could listen long enough to know what the talk was about. Roberto hadn't asked him about Zeke's messages yet, but he didn't want to be embarrassed if and when that time came.

Zeke left his easel at the side of the stage, and instead carried a spool of fishing line in his hands. He tied the end to one leg of the table holding the decorated box as he spoke. "This week, we've talked about the words we say that reflect what's in our heart. We've also talked about pride and arrogance, anger and jealousy. Tonight, I thought we'd focus on lying and deceit. Have you ever walked into a spider web? You try to back away or get out of it, but it only seems to make things worse?" He waved his arms to mimic someone entangled in a spider web. "A nineteenth century author named Sir Walter Scott wrote, 'Oh, what a tangled web we weave when first we practice to deceive.' Lying is a lot like a spider weaving a web. You tell a little lie, nothing big, but then you have to tell another one to cover it up. Pretty soon, that lie isn't enough so you tell another one. But now, you can't remember exactly what you said in the very first lie."

While he talked, Zeke wove the fishing line in and around the other table legs so it crisscrossed itself several times. "I chose fishing line here for a reason. I could've used yarn or thread. But many times, our deceit is invisible at first, at least to other people."

Taylor craned his neck to see as Zeke summoned a couple of campers from the front row to the stage, positioning them on either side of the table. One tried to peek inside the box but Zeke wound the nylon line over and under the box, then around each of the campers until they were both so entangled in the fishing line, they couldn't move their arms or legs. *A nice change from the drawing, but I need to get out and get some worms...* He grinned. What would Luke's reaction be to a worm crawling up his leg? How could he make Luke think it was a snake?

Taylor went over his plan again. Of course, he'd have to lie a little, but this was merely a joke. A harmless prank wasn't really deceit, was it? He squirmed and eyed the door.

Zeke seemed to take forever to make his point, but at last, he concluded with, "What's in your heart?" and a prayer.

Taylor wasted no time. A second after the final amen, he bolted through the door. Outside, he slowed to a more normal pace. *Take it easy.* Make it look like you've got all the time in the world. He meandered from one shadow to the next until he was

certain no other campers were close enough to see him. Afraid
the flashlight might give him away, he stumbled a couple times
before his eyes adjusted to the darkness. When he reached the
marshy area Nurse Willie had mentioned, he peered up the hill.
Figures moved toward the cabins, their voices carried by the
night air. Taylor could make out a word or two, but most of it was
unintelligible. He turned his back to them and squatted close to
the ground before turning on his flashlight. The beam swept back
and forth over the soft ground. His feet sank into the dirt if he
stayed too long in one place, but when he tried to move, the
suction nearly pulled off his flip-flops. Taylor muttered.

"C'mon, c'mon. I don't have all night."

At last, he spotted a nightcrawler trying to wriggle back into
the earth. He yanked it from the ground, but only half of it came
up in his hand. His lip curled in disgust and he dropped it.
Finding another one still wholly above ground, he snatched it up.
It wiggled and squirmed, smearing mud on his hand. At least, he
hoped it was mud and not something else.

Moving on, he spotted another worm burrowing into the
earth. This time, his fingers gently tugged it from the ground.
Two! He should've brought the dish Willie gave him. These
things were so big, two nearly filled his hand. He needed to hurry.
The only voices he heard now were muffled within the cabins. He
had to get back soon, before Harris or anyone else noticed he was
missing.

Taylor widened his search until he discovered two more night
crawlers. He'd hoped for six, but these four were already a good
handful. And he still had to get them into the cabin without
anyone noticing.

Taylor flicked off his flashlight, stuck it under his arm and
raced up the hill to the cabin. At the last minute, he swerved to
approach the cabin from the direction of the chapel, just in case
anyone saw him coming. Before opening the door, he wrangled
his fist into his pocket, still loosely cupping the worms. The

screen door slammed behind him as he sauntered into the bunkroom.

Steven was messing around with his suitcase, laying out his clothes for the next day. *Weird, but maybe that's what blind people do.* Luke sat on his bed, yukking it up with the guys on the other side.

How to sneak the worms into Luke's sleeping bag without getting caught?

Taylor couldn't keep his hand in his pocket all night. What if they turned into a stinky, slimy mess right there, before he had a chance to slip them out?

Luke stood up, toothbrush in hand. He glanced at Taylor on his way to the bathroom, an irritating smirk pulling his lips to one side.

Let's see if you're still smirking later on, Puke.

While Taylor searched for an excuse to get close enough to deposit his treasure in Luke's bunk, one of the boys whacked his friend with a pillow, knocking him onto Luke's bed and pushing the bottom of the unzipped sleeping bag off the side of the bed.

Perfect.

When the boys resumed their fight elsewhere, Taylor snatched Steven's swim trunks which hung on the cross bar at the end of his bed. They were still damp from the afternoon's swim. Hiding them behind his left leg, Taylor crouched between Steven's and Luke's beds and pretended to lift them from the floor.

"Hey, Steven, are these your swim shorts?" He held them out to Steven while his other hand slid inside Luke's sleeping bag and released the nightcrawlers.

Steven took his shorts and felt along the decorative stitching and the seams. "Yeah. Where were they?"

"I picked them up off the floor."

Steven looked puzzled. "How'd they get down there? I know I hung them up."

"Someone probably knocked them off when they walked by."
Taylor turned to the boys engaged in the pillow fight. "Hey, watch
what you're doing. You're messing up other people's stuff. Look at
this." He shook the corner of the sleeping bag so it lay squarely
on the bed again then asked Steven, "Want me to hang them back
up for you?"

Steven held them out. "Yeah, thanks."

"No problem." Taylor rolled his lips in to suppress a smile.
Now to plant the thought of snakes in Luke's mind. He rubbed his
muddy hand on his beach towel, then squirted a dab of tooth-
paste onto his toothbrush and entered the bathroom. Moving
along the wall, he bent over as if examining the baseboard.

Luke peered at him through the mirror's reflection. "What are
you doing?"

Taylor glanced at Luke, but continued his examination. "I
don't think you want to know."

Luke spun around. "Let me decide that. What are you
looking at?"

"No, really. Trust me. You do not want to know." Taylor's gaze
traveled along the baseboard from the bathroom door all the way
to the other end.

Luke huffed and shuffled toward the door. "You're just being
stupid."

Taylor murmured to himself. "I thought for sure I saw one of
those little snakes crawling along here. Guess I must've imagined
it."

Luke practically leaped through the door. Some of the other
boys in the bathroom joined the search, but they found nothing.

Harris soon called everyone for devotions and Taylor came
out of the bathroom to find Luke on the farthest couch, feet
tucked up underneath his crossed legs.

Taylor bit his lip to keep from laughing. What a hoot this was
going to be. As long as Luke didn't smoosh the worms before they
had a chance to crawl up his legs. He crossed his fingers they'd

survive inside the sleeping bag. For now, the cabin was too warm with the day's accumulated heat. It would take a couple hours to cool off enough to slip inside a sleeping bag. But Taylor intended to stay awake for this, no matter how early he'd been up this morning.

12

L uke's cry woke everyone in the cabin, including Taylor. Not quite a scream, but definitely more than a yell. Luke fell to the floor with a thump and continued a battle with his sleeping bag.

Steven raised himself on one elbow. "Luke? Are you dreaming? What's wrong?"

Taylor sat up in bed, straining to see the cause of the muffled thumps and bumps coming from the other side of Steven's bunk. What had he missed by falling asleep?

Harris appeared in the doorway, silhouetted by the light from his room. "What's going on?" He frowned at Luke. "What are you doing?"

Luke thrashed, barely able to get the words out. "S-s- snake. In my bag. Let me out!"

Harris flipped the cabin lights on, prompting groans of protest from the rest of the boys. He took hold of Luke's sleeping bag, untwisted it and held it taut while Luke scrambled out.

"It was slithering up my leg." Luke backed up, flattening himself against the wall, then hopped onto his bed. "I felt it. I felt it." He shivered and ran his hands up and down his legs as if wiping something off.

"How would a snake get into your sleeping bag?" Harris laid the bag flat on the floor and pulled the top back. "I don't see any snake."

Luke pointed to a spot about two-thirds down from the top of the bag, his voice nearly hysterical. "There! Right there!"

Harris took a closer look. "That's a worm, a nightcrawler." He picked it up and let it dangle from his finger. "And a half-dead one at that."

"There's another one!"

Harris picked up the second one and examined the bag more closely. "Hmm. You'll want to wash this out tomorrow. Looks like you laid on a couple. They're smashed."

The kid on the top bunk leaned over the edge of his bed. "Let's see it!"

"Eeuww." The kid in the bottom bunk on the other side of Luke curled his lip.

Another kid threw the top of his sleeping bag aside and curled his legs up close to his body. "I think I feel something in my bag." Others checked their bags as well and Taylor followed along, pretending to thoroughly check his sleeping bag.

Harris picked up Luke's bag, shook it outside the front door and returned it to Luke. "Just turn it inside out. You'll be fine." He switched the lights off again and yawned as he headed into his room. "Everybody go back to sleep. No talking."

Taylor snickered to himself. The pure terror on Luke's face was so much more appealing than his usual cocky expression. He turned over and snuggled his face into the pillow to muffle his laughter. Sleep would come, eventually. For him anyway. Luke probably wouldn't get any sleep at all. Maybe not for the rest of the week.

TAYLOR PUSHED his tray along the buffet line Thursday morning. Getting up for breakfast was rough after being awakened in the middle of the night. He chuckled to himself remembering Luke's reaction to the worms.

Hmm. What to eat? Oatmeal? No way. Eggs and bacon? Definitely the bacon. And a mound of sugar-frosted flakes in his bowl. He snagged a couple cartons of milk and looked for a table. Nick was already sitting with Claire, Steven and Brady so Taylor joined them, setting his tray on the table in time to hear Steven's version of last night's excitement.

Claire scooted over to make room for Taylor. "Did you see all this, too?"

"I couldn't see him wrestling with his sleeping bag, but I heard him hit the floor in it. He practically ran into the wall when he finally got out of it, and then he bounced back onto his bed " Laughter choked out the rest of what he meant to say.

Claire giggled. "Why was he so scared of a few worms?"

Steven was laughing, too. "He thought it was a snake."

Brady's chuckle turned to a grimace. "A snake?"

Claire shuddered. "Why would he think that?"

"He's terrified of snakes." Taylor dumped one carton of milk on his cereal. He'd save the bacon for last. "We saw a little one the other night during the counselor hunt and he ran like someone dropped a firecracker in his shorts."

Brady's eyes narrowed. "So, who put the worms in his bed?"

Claire's gaze swiveled from Brady to Steven to Taylor. "Taylor?" She drew his name out.

Shrugging, Taylor pushed soggy cereal around the bowl with his spoon. "I admit I might have planted the snake idea in his mind when I thought I saw a snake crawl into the bathroom."

"For real?" Brady asked. "In the bathroom?"

Claire grimaced. A shiver shook her hunched shoulders.

Taylor rolled his bottom lip in. "Let's just say there was nothing there when I looked."

"O-oh, that's mean." Claire's dimples appeared as she and Brady exchanged knowing grins.

"What are we doing for rec today?" Taylor asked. "I forgot to look before I came in here."

"Ka-joe-bee can-can?" Claire pronounced each syllable. "I guess that's how you say it. Do you know what it is?"

"Never heard of it." Taylor raised the bowl to his mouth. The sugary milk left over from the cereal was the best part. A rough slap on his back splashed the milk up his nose, down his neck and chest. He blew out his nostrils and dropped the bowl to the table, sloshing what was left of the milk onto the table. Beside him, Marissa stifled a giggle.

"Need a napkin, Taybo?"

Luke snorted from behind and Taylor jumped to his feet to face him. "What'd you do that for?"

Luke's smile evaporated. His jaw hardened and his eyes narrowed. "That's for last night."

"What are you blaming me for? You're the one who freaked out over a couple of worms."

Marissa squinted at Taylor, then Luke. "What are you guys talking about?"

Luke crowded Taylor against the table, chest to chest.

"If you ever go near my stuff again, I'll make you so sorry."

Taylor shoved him back. Luke lunged and grabbed Taylor's wet t-shirt in his fists.

Marissa yanked on Luke's arm. "Leave him alone. What is wrong with you two? Stop it."

Voices from the surrounding tables grew quiet. Whispers of a fight rustled through the air until Luke backed off. He glared at Taylor.

"You'll pay for this. I promise you're gonna pay."

Taylor tugged at his shirt to straighten it and glared right back. "Ooh, I'm scared. But look! I'm not running away screaming like a big sissy."

Luke lunged again. More than one chair scraped the floor behind Taylor. Suddenly, Brady stood at Taylor's shoulder.

"Cut it out, Luke," Claire ordered.

Eyes wide, Marissa grabbed Luke's arm and pulled. "Leave him alone. C'mon. Let's go."

Luke allowed her to lead him away, but every few steps, he tossed a dagger-glance back over his shoulder. Taylor's breathing slowed to normal after they left the dining hall. He turned back to the table where Steven and Claire were both standing at alert. Milk dripped onto his chair. His damp shirt stuck to his chest. Claire handed him her napkin, then got up to grab more from the condiments nook. Taylor made a quick swipe at the spilled milk. Claire returned and helped sop up the milk.

"He is such a jerk."

Brady added Steven's napkin to the cleanup effort. "Yeah, just like someone I knew last year." He eyed Taylor.

Steven sucked in a slow breath. Claire's hand froze. She shot nervous glances between Taylor and Brady. Taylor threw the dripping napkins onto his tray. He didn't need this from Brady, especially not now. He faced him, jaw set.

"I said last year." A corner of Brady's mouth turned up. "This year's different." Not a hint of challenge showed in Brady's expression.

No condemnation. No hostility. Somewhere deep inside, a pinprick of guilt stabbed Taylor's gut. Brady wasn't trying to pick a fight like Luke.

Taylor swallowed the angry words on his tongue, picked up his tray and headed for the exit. Last year, he'd made Brady's life miserable—insulting him, teasing him, dumping him out of his canoe, along with Steven and Claire, to keep them from winning a race. They had every right to hold a grudge, but instead they stood up, ready to fight for him. No one had ever done that before.

G‌UILT NIBBLED at Taylor's gut all morning, and the Bible study about King Ahab didn't help. Ahab wanted a vineyard, but the owner refused to sell it to him. Ahab went home and pouted until his wife, the evil queen Jezebel, got the vineyard for him. She framed the owner for something he didn't do and put him to death. Poor guy. Just because the king envied his vineyard.

Envy. Jealousy.

The truth hit him like a chilly, early morning dip in the lake. He might as well be Ahab. He'd tormented Brady because of the attention he got for playing his trumpet so well. And he'd envied Brady's friendship with Steven and Claire. That was last year, but was this year any different? Was he really picking on Luke because of his cocky attitude? That was part of it, but if he were honest, he envied Luke's driver's license and his hot car. After what Dad said to him on Sunday, Luke's bragging about his dad giving him the 'Vette was more than Taylor could stand. He folded his arms tight across his chest, but it did nothing to quell the ache inside. What should he do now? The weird feeling in his stomach told him something had to change, and that something was most likely him.

T‌HREE WAIST-HIGH ALUMINUM garbage cans dotted the open rec field like points of a triangle, each about ten yards from the others. A counselor stood in the middle and called out instructions.

"Welcome to Kajobe Can-Can. I need everyone to form a circle around the outside of the garbage cans, alternating team members. Do not stand next to a member of your own team."

Another counselor handed out a two-foot length of heavy

rope to each camper. The ropes were knotted at both ends. Taylor tried several different grips on the sturdy rope in his hand.

"Any of you ever play this before?" The counselor in the center looked around the circle. Only a few hands went up.

"Okay. Your right hand should be holding one end of your rope inside the knot. With your left hand, grab the other end of your neighbor's rope. Again, hold it inside the knot. There shouldn't be any breaks in the circle." She waited until everyone was connected all the way around. "When I blow the whistle, start moving to your left around the cans. Your goal is to avoid any kind of contact with a garbage can. At the same time, you'll try to force members of the other team to come into contact with the garbage cans. A pinky-touch or even if a part of your clothing touches a can, you're out of the game. Also, if you lose your grip or let go of the rope at any time during active play, you're out. Any questions?"

Taylor glanced across the circle at Claire. Head down, feet apart, arms out to the sides gripping the ropes, she looked like a boxer preparing to enter the ring. He imagined her wearing a mouth guard, breathing hard through her nostrils. Seeing him, she smiled slightly and raised her eyebrows. He returned the smile. *Good luck to you, too.*

The counselor finished. "Whenever anyone gets cut, we'll take a time-out to regroup. The last team standing wins. Everybody ready?"

A roar went up from the circle. "Yeah!"

The counselor blew her whistle and the circle moved clockwise.

Taylor backed away from the garbage can. Let the others play first. If he followed along and watched, maybe he could come up with a strategy for winning. Ahead of him, a section of the circle swayed toward a can and one of his team members missed it by an inch, avoiding it by turning sideways at the last minute.

On his right, the circle pulled back, stretching his arms in opposite directions. His little fingers pinched against the knots in the ropes. Taylor struggled to pull his arms in, but one minute he was pulled forward, the next sideways, then backward. Simply staying on his feet was a challenge. If he stumbled, they could pull him right into one of the cans.

Like a swarm of gnats, the circle shifted, constantly changing shape and direction. The younger, weaker kids left the game first, running into a can or losing their grip on the rope. Each time-out, Taylor tightened his grip and pulled his elbows in close. Adrenaline pumped through his body in anticipation of the whistle to resume the game. How much longer could he avoid the cans?

The whistle sounded and his side of the tightening circle surged toward one of the garbage cans. Opponents on either side dragged Taylor closer, closer. His shoulders burned from the strain as he was pulled within feet of the can. A backward feint, then he sprinted forward, spreading his legs wide as he leaped over the can. *Made it!* But as soon as he landed, he was pulled backward. At the last minute, Taylor sidestepped the can, missing it by a hair.

Now the other side surged. Claire's strength was no match for the bigger guys, but Taylor could almost see the wheels turning in her head. No doubt she was scheming a way to outsmart them. If only he could help her out. Facing off on opposite sides of a can with a heavy guy on her left, Claire dropped her hand down close to the can. A flick of her wrist and a sharp tug scraped her opponent's hand across the rim of the can. He threw his end of the rope at her and stalked away, muttering in a disgusted tone.

The circle was shrinking. A counselor removed one of the garbage cans and started the game again. Taylor's biceps ached. His palms burned from the twisting and pulling of the rope, but nothing hurt as bad as his little fingers smashed up against the knots. Sweat dampened his hair and dripped from his nose as he twisted and juked like a football player. He and a teammate dragged the opponent between them to the can. *Out.*

Taylor looked for Claire. She was still in the game. They circled the cans again and again, losing players until two opponents and a teammate separated him from Claire on each side. One opponent lost his grip, and the circle was reduced to seven players around one can. Cleats would've helped a lot right now, but who brings cleats to camp?

Claire caught his eye. She glanced to her left. The briefest shake of her head signaled an attack on the opponent to her left. But when the whistle sounded, the opponents on either side yanked her forward, straight in to the can. Claire skirted it like a batter avoiding a pitch, only to be pulled back toward it.

Taylor leaned hard to the left, his weight throwing off their opponents' strategy. Claire edged around the can and tugged the opponent on her right into it.

Three against three now. A single rope separated Taylor from his other teammate, but Claire had opponents on both sides of her. She looked ragged. Sweat glued her t-shirt to her ribs. Her arms and shoulders sagged. Taylor jutted his chin at her. *Keep going. Stay strong.* She inhaled deeply, adjusted her grip on the ropes and nodded.

The game resumed, catching Taylor's teammate off guard. He hit the can and dropped out. Three opponents— two boys and a girl—against Taylor and Claire. Could he and Claire stand? Doubtful. All around them, the kids who'd been eliminated shouted and cheered on their remaining players.

Claire's eyes flicked back and forth between Taylor and their female opponent.

No.

Taylor cut his eyes to the guy on her left. Claire frowned. Taylor flexed his aching biceps, flinching at the pain. *Take out the strongest guy first.* Did she get the message? No time to wonder. Game on.

The circle rotated clockwise. In two running steps, Taylor leap-frogged over the can, jerking sharp left upon landing. Claire pulled to her right, forcing the two opponents backward. They split around the can, but the girl lost her balance and fell against it. Out.

Two against two. Every part of Taylor's body hurt, from his little fingers to his arms, up his shoulders and neck. Even his legs ached from the strain of resistance. If he was this wasted, how could Claire even remain standing? Would her strength hold up? They squared off, an opponent between them on each side, the ropes taut between them. At the whistle, Taylor jerked left. The opponent on his right leaped over the can and with help from his teammate, forced Taylor backward toward the garbage can. Claire countered, throwing her weight to the side to pull Taylor past the can. One opponent tried a back-jump over the can. His leg caught the rim.

Claire grinned at Taylor, new light shining in her eyes. They just might win.

13

Taylor shook his arms, rolled his shoulders, and readied himself for another round. Hopefully, their last.

The three players circled, so close now that any sudden move could send one or all of them right into the garbage can. Taylor sped up, careful not to pull Claire too fast while pushing the guy ahead of him. The kid yanked Taylor's rope, tipping him off balance, then switched direction. Taylor recovered, met Claire's gaze and they both pulled back, yanking hard on their ropes. The guy nosedived into the can.

The counselor's whistle blew.

"Winners!"

Cheers filled the air and their team flocked around them. Taylor tried to release his grip on the ropes, but they were too stiff to respond. His little fingers had gone numb.

Claire pried her fingers away from the rope and lifted a rigid hand to massage her upper arm with her palm. "I'd give you a high five, but it hurts to raise my arm."

Taylor held out his stiff, cupped hand for a fist bump.

Claire barely tapped her knuckles to his. "I think my little fingers are permanently injured, and those ropes scraped my hands raw!" She held her palms out for his inspection.

Their last opponent walked past and Taylor couldn't resist. "Too bad, loser."

The kid scowled at him.

Claire dropped her hands to her side. "Why do you do that?" She regarded him with a mix of disappointment and disapproval.

"Do what?"

"Say mean things like that."

Taylor's mouth pulled to the side and he rolled his eyes.

"The way Marissa brags about you either she's never heard you talk like that or she lives in a dream world."

Taylor hunched his shoulders and looked away. Yeah, Rissa lived in Fantasyland, where everything was fun and rosy. Kind of like his dream of racing cars. Maybe that's why she believed in his dream when no one else did.

Claire started toward the cabins, following the others. She stopped and turned toward him. "Hey, remember when you asked me if she'd been out late? Tuesday night, she must have snuck out after the rest of us were asleep. She woke me up trying to get back in."

"I know." Taylor caught up with her. "She and Luke went for a midnight swim." He flexed his hands as the feeling returned to his fingers. "I made her go back to the cabin before she got caught."

Claire caught her breath. "You did? You were out, too?"

"I had a feeling Luke was meeting her when I heard him sneaking out. So I followed him down to the lake and surprised them."

"Well, I'm glad you guys didn't get caught."

Taylor glanced sideways at her. "They didn't get caught. I did."

Claire halted. She tipped her head to the side. "Wait. They snuck out. You followed to make Marissa to go back to the cabin and you're the only one who got caught? Did Zeke punish you?"

"Zeke and Harris both." Taylor shrugged and kept walking. "Nothing new. Happens all the time at home."

Claire hurried up to him, pulling on his arm until he stopped. "Do you always take the blame when Marissa gets into trouble?"

Taylor nodded. "Pretty much." He shifted under Claire's steady gaze and looked away.

"No wonder she adores you."

TAYLOR LEANED over the driver's seat to tighten a bolt on the floor. Sweat dripped from his nose onto the carpet. A fan would've made things more comfortable as he and Roberto replaced the back seat and now the front bucket seats. Or moving the car out of the garage would've let them catch a breeze, at least. He pulled the front of his t-shirt up and wiped the sweat from his face before it dripped onto the new seat cover. The leather added a real touch of class to the car.

Roberto grinned at him from the passenger side. "Looks good, no?"

"Looks great!" Taylor admired the interior.

Roberto held out his keys. "Start her up. Let's see how they feel." He sat on the passenger seat.

Taylor twisted around and settled into the driver's seat, adjusting it forward an inch or two. His foot pressed the gas pedal once and he turned the key. The engine rumbled to life.

Roberto tested the passenger seat with a slight bouncing motion. "Is good, huh? Comfortable, si?"

"Yeah, I like the new cushions. And the covers look awesome. Can we take her out now?"

Roberto shook his head. "Is not ready."

What's not ready? Couldn't they at least take it out around the parking lot? He'd never get to see what it was like on the road before camp ended. Taylor closed his eyes and drank in the sound. The purr of the engine vibrated to his fingers around the steering wheel. His imagination ran free—driving along the highway, windows down, wind blowing his hair back, cooling his neck.

A tap on his arm brought him back to the garage where Roberto offered him a can of root beer. That's what his dream was missing, a cold drink in one hand. But for now, he'd better not risk spilling soda on Roberto's new seat. He cut the engine and looked through the windshield to see another car make a quick circle in front of the shed. It came to an abrupt stop in front of the open bay door. The driver's door flew open and Janie jumped out.

"It's Gabriella. She's already at the hospital." She left the car running and hurried around to the passenger side. "We need to go now!"

Roberto started for Janie's car, then doubled back, holding out his soda can. Taylor scrambled from the Mustang and took the can from him. Roberto headed back to Janie's car, only to turn around again and pull a wrench from his back pocket. He tossed it onto the worktable.

"Roberto, come on. Hurry!" Janie stamped her foot beside the open passenger door.

Roberto scurried out to the car. He called to Taylor over his shoulder. "You will close up, por favor? Lock everything?"

"I will." Taylor grinned at Roberto's frenzied back and forth dash between the car and the garage. Who'd have thought he could move that fast? "Don't worry. I'll put everything away and lock it all up. Go on! You're going to be a grampa!"

A smile broke out on Roberto's leathery face as he stuck one foot in the car. "Abuelo! I be un abuelo." Both car doors slammed. Roberto gunned the engine and they sped away from the shed, tires squealing.

Taylor chuckled and set the soda can on the worktable. He opened his and downed half of it, then waited for the belch. Buurraaaap! He patted his stomach. That felt good.

Roberto's unopened soda went back into the cooler, his wrench in the toolbox. Taylor leaned into the Mustang to retrieve the wrench he'd used and saw the keys dangling from the ignition. He grabbed them and raced outside to catch Roberto, but the car was long gone. Maybe halfway to the hospital by now.

Taylor fingered the keys, studying them as he went back into the garage. Should he leave them here or take them with him when he locked up? Roberto usually kept them in his pocket rather than leave them in the garage. A few other keys jingled on the ring as well. Maybe one unlocked the side door? He walked over and tried the different keys until he found one that worked. In that case, he'd better not leave them locked inside the garage. Tomorrow morning, he'd go to breakfast early and hand the keys over to Janie.

Taylor made sure the side door was locked then retrieved his soda. He took another gulp of the chilled soda and let his gaze wander over the Mustang. What was left to fix? He flirted with the temptation to take it out around the parking lot. He sat in the driver's seat again, inserted the key in the ignition. One hand atop the steering wheel, he peered out the windshield at an imaginary road. His foot pressed the accelerator pedal to the floor and let it up. He twisted the key, bringing the engine to life. His right hand moved to the gearshift.

Was it possible to want something so bad it was almost a physical ache? Taylor pressed the accelerator, his heartbeat racing along with the revving of the engine. The tachometer needle bobbed higher, higher. His eyes closed and once more, he was out on the open road. No, this time he was at a stoplight, challenging Luke in his Corvette. Their engines roared in competition. The light changed to green and he stomped on the accelerator, shooting out ahead of Luke.

He shook his head. *That'll never happen, but it's fun to dream.*

Opening his eyes, he noticed Luke standing in the doorway. Still dreaming? He blinked. No, Luke was real. The smirk should've been a clue; he'd never allow the Pukester to wear a lousy sneer like that in his dreams.

Taylor shut the car off. "What are you doing here?"

"This where you've been hiding every evening, skipping out of group Rec?" Luke sauntered over to the car, giving it a once over as if it were a hot chick. He worked his way from front to back, peeking inside.

Taylor pulled the keys and got out of the car. "Time for evening worship. I was just closing up."

"Liar." Luke's eyes dropped to the keys in Taylor's hand. "You've got the keys. Let's take her out. I bet she runs sweet."

Taylor's fingers curled around Roberto's keys. Luke had no clue how tempting his idea was. They could do a quick run around the parking lot. No one would know. And maybe it would shut Luke's mouth.

"Come on. Let's go." Luke opened the passenger door, but Taylor didn't move. "What's the matter? You scared? This little pony too much for you to handle?"

Taylor sucked in a breath and shoved the keys in his pocket. "It's not ready to drive yet." He turned off the garage lights and reached for the button to close the overhead door. "Time to get out of here."

The bell rang for evening worship. Luke scowled and slammed the door shut. "You're just chicken, scared of the old man. He doesn't have to know." He laughed, but without humor. "What could he do even if he did find out?"

Taylor's jaw clenched and his fingers balled into a fist. Luke stepped out of the garage. Taylor pressed the button, ducking under the descending door. Luke waited, making no sign of leaving. Taylor wasn't about to leave him here, even with the place locked up. "Aren't you going to evening worship?"

"Yep, right after you." Luke motioned for Taylor to lead the way.

Taylor started for the chapel, his blood sizzling. If Zeke had asked what was in his heart at the moment, he'd have to say hatred. Seeing Luke in the garage shattered his dream and fouled the whole place. That car had been his escape this week, the garage the only place he could go and not have to think about Luke or Marissa or Claire or anything else. Luke's opinion of pony cars had been clear from Day One. So why the sudden interest in Roberto's Mustang?

Taylor entered the chapel and threw himself into a seat next to Brady and Steven. They acknowledged him, but continued their conversation. Luke continued on to where Marissa was sitting and plopped down beside her. The worship band finished warming up and everyone stood to join in singing the first song.

Taylor rose too, but the image of Luke peering at him from the garage entrance replayed over and over in his mind, along with some ugly words.

Chicken. Scared of the old man.

Yeah, he was scared, but not the way Luke meant. Taylor hated the thought of disappointing Roberto, and not just because of the Mustang. Roberto accepted him, never made him feel stupid or worthless. Nobody at home trusted him with anything, but Roberto left him to close up the garage and take care of the car. As hard as it was to have the keys in his hand and not take it out for a test runif Roberto said it wasn't ready, he'd believe him.

The band finished their last song, and Taylor and the rest of the campers sat down. Zeke stood next to the jeweled box, resting one arm atop the lid.

"What's in your heart? I've asked you that over and over this week. Have you discovered things you didn't know were there? Did you find things you don't want anyone to know about? Things you wouldn't want exposed?" He opened the lid of the box and pulled out a two-liter bottle filled with a dirty-looking liquid, holding it up for everyone to see. "Have you ever seen what comes out of the tap after the water's been turned off for a while? It usually looks like this." Zeke shook the bottle and the brown water swirled around inside. "When the water is turned back on, it gushes through the pipes, pushing out the sediment that has collected there. Anyone care to drink this?"

"Eeuw!" The campers voiced their disgust. "No!"

Taylor wrinkled his nose.

Zeke strolled down the aisle, giving everyone a closer look at the unappetizing water in the jar. "Would you wash your hands in this? What about your clothes?" He turned around and walked to the front of the chapel again. "'Out of the overflow of the heart, the mouth speaks.' The water in this bottle symbolizes the words that come from your mouth. If you wouldn't drink it, wash with it, or do your laundry in it, why should it come out of your mouth? Why permit dirty, disgusting and unhealthy words and thoughts to dwell in your heart?"

Zeke set the bottle on the table in front of the box. He reached inside again and this time, he pulled out a black balloon that had yet to be inflated. "Is your heart puffed up with pride?" He took a deep breath and blew into the balloon until it reached softball size. "Are you arrogant, with an inflated sense of your own importance?" He blew into it again, until the balloon was fat and round.

Taylor inhaled and exhaled along with Zeke. Before long, the balloon looked about to burst and Zeke held it high in the air.

"The Bible warns us to think soberly about our own worth and abilities, and to consider others as better than ourselves. That doesn't fit with the general attitude of our competitive culture. Being puffed up with pride may not seem like a dangerous thing but, at some point, the bubble will burst. It might be a slow leak." Zeke pinched and stretched the balloon's neck until it let out a high-pitched squeal. "Or sometimes, it happens all at once." He released the balloon. It zoomed crazily over the first two rows before falling to the aisle floor. "What's in your heart?"

Again, Zeke reached into the box. This time when he pulled out his hand, it was covered with green slime, the kind Taylor had made in grade school with detergent and glue. The director caught the drips with his other hand.

"What about jealousy and anger? Does jealousy seep into your relationships like mold that sickens and destroys? Does your anger get the best of you, so that it controls you more often than you control it? What's in your heart?"

Zeke scraped the slime from his hands into a bowl that sat next to the bottle of dirty water. He wiped his hand on a towel, and once more withdrew something from the box. A mask. No, two masks. One was a clown face, the other a grotesque old man.

"Has lying and deceitfulness found a place in your heart? Does lying come easier than telling the truth? Or maybe you're hiding behind a face you want the world to see." He held up the clown mask, then raised the ugly one. "Do you play the clown or the tough guy to keep people from seeing what's really inside, to mask some deep hurt and keep it from showing?"

Taylor crossed his arms, sliding his fingers between his arms and his ribs. His gaze dropped to the floor. Jealousy wasn't his only problem. It was all there inside, everything Zeke talked about—the things he said to other kids, lying, deceit, pride, anger. Could he change? Give all that up? He glanced at Luke and answered his own question. *Not yet.*

Zeke dismissed them, and Taylor walked with Brady and Steven back to the cabins. He was glad Steven kept up a steady monologue so he didn't have to say much. Brady veered off to his cabin and Taylor guided Steven into their cabin and the bunkroom. He checked his pocket again, feeling the lumpy, jagged outline of Roberto's keys before dropping his shorts on the heap of clothes atop his duffle bag. He wouldn't have to get up for another torture session with Harris tomorrow morning, but he'd need to hit the dining hall early to give Roberto's keys to Janie.

Luke entered the bunkroom. The sight of him still got Taylor's blood pumping. He dug out his magazine and paged through it to avoid the smirky looks Luke kept throwing at him. Even during devotions, the Puke grinned like he was keeping a secret. Planning to sneak out again to meet Marissa?

Good luck, Riss. I won't be there to bail you out this time. You're on your own.

With two minutes to go until lights out, Taylor hurried to the bathroom to brush his teeth.

Luke stood at the first sink, his mouth curving into a foamy grin when he saw Taylor. He spit and rinsed his mouth, tapped his toothbrush against the sink and spoke to Taylor's image in the mirror. "How about we go for a ride tonight after everyone's asleep?"

Taylor ignored him, continuing to brush his teeth until his gums grew sore. When would the guy leave?

Hands on the counter, Luke leaned closer and wheedled. "Come on, I dare ya. Just around the parking lot. We'll have it back in the garage before anyone even knows we're out."

Taylor leaned over to spit, fighting the urge to spew in Luke's face. He rinsed his toothbrush and swiped his mouth a couple times before replying. "It's not ready to drive yet."

"What's not ready? You're just scared of the old man." Luke clucked like a chicken.

"And you're an idiot." Taylor pushed him aside and left the bathroom, gritting his teeth against the cackling noise Luke made behind him. The jerk. What does Marissa see in the guy?

14

dare, huh? You'll see. I'm not scared of Roberto or anyone else.

The metal key cooled Taylor's hot fingers. The ignition caught, sending a thrill up his spine as the engine rumbled to life. His foot pressed the accelerator and he revved the engine once, twice. He smiled at the Mustang's throaty roar. Ready, set, go! He stomped the accelerator to the floor and the car leaped forward.

Wait! The garage door's not open!

Taylor jerked upright in bed, eyes wide open, but seeing little in the sparse moonlight that made its way into the cabin. He gulped air into his lungs and waited for his heart to throttle back to idle speed. Sweat trickled down his chest. He expelled a breath and flopped back onto his pillow. Just a dream, but it was so real —the turn of the key, the pressure of the accelerator, the rumble of the engine.

Somewhere in the night, an engine growled, bringing Taylor upright again. This time, he was awake and that sound was real. Why would Roberto be working this late at night? It had to be well past midnight. And how did he get the key? A spare, maybe?

Taylor glanced at Luke's bunk. Empty. He scrambled out of bed, groping for his shorts. Where are they? He'd left them right there on top of his other clothes, but now they weren't there. He tossed t-shirts and other items onto the bed, then stood up and looked all around. A dark lump of something lay in the bunkroom doorway. His shorts maybe? He went over and picked them up. How did they get over here?

Taylor stepped into them, feeling for the keys in the pocket. He thrust his hand deep inside then patted the other pockets. No keys. His heart took off like a racecar in the home stretch. He dashed out the door, letting it slam behind him, and sprinted toward the garage. His bare feet stung from hitting stones and twigs hidden in the darkness, but he didn't stop until he reached the edge of the parking lot. Except for an occasional lightning bug, all was dark, the bay doors closed. The camp pick-up truck was parked off to one side as usual. Had he imagined it? Maybe Roberto had been there, but he'd closed up and gone home. Taylor stepped closer, his senses on high alert as he peered through the moonlit darkness, looking for anything out of the ordinary.

Vrrooomm.

The garage door did little to muffle the sound that nearly lifted him off his feet. The bay door rose, its rollers grating in their tracks. Headlights flicked on, illuminating a figure scurrying around to the passenger's side. Marissa!

The car door slammed. If Rissa's in the passenger seat, Luke must be driving. The motor revved and the car charged out of the garage, tires squealing.

"No-o-oo!" Taylor ran toward the car, waving his arms in the air. The car jerked away from him, making a sharp turn into the parking lot before it swerved drunkenly onto the road that wound through camp.

"Marissa!" Taylor followed them on foot, but the car was going way too fast. He gasped, unable to close his eyes as the car came within inches of sideswiping a tree. The engine protested a downshift and the car slowed, but its speed was still too high for the narrow, winding service road. He'd never catch up chasing them, but maybe if he cut across camp. The road angled around behind the girls' cabins and ended at the boat launch.

Taylor reached the road behind the girls' cabins as the Mustang approached. He stood in the middle of it, waving his hands. "Stop! Stop!"

The headlights blinded him and he jumped out of the way at the last second, the car barreling past him toward the lake. Marissa's screams rose above the engine noise, and Taylor swore. He had to stop them, had to keep Marissa from getting hurt. *Why doesn't he just cut the motor?*

The car crashed through the boat launch gate with a sickening crunch, then splashed into the lake. The sound stole Taylor's breath away. Dizziness threatened to knock him over, and he choked back the nausea that clawed up his throat. The car's engine died in the water. Taylor's heart nearly exploded in his chest.

Sudden silence sent him sprinting down to the shore. Light from the full moon revealed the car at an angle with its nose in the lake. Water splashed the black stripes atop its hood.

Luke emerged from the driver's seat and bent over, looking back into the car. "Come on! Quit crying and let's get out of here before we get caught."

Taylor splashed toward Luke, but Marissa's sobs drew him to her side of the car. Through the open window, he glimpsed his sister leaning forward, head in her hands. He screamed across the roof at Luke. "What have you done? You "

"It doesn't have any brakes! Why didn't you tell me this piece of junk couldn't stop?" Luke sloshed through the water to the rear of the car.

"I told you it wasn't ready to drive." Taylor shouted as his gaze swept the car from front to back. "You won't get away with this. You are going to pay big time."

Luke laughed. "Me? Guess again, fool. Who had the keys in his pocket?" He splashed water onto the car's trunk. "Marissa, you coming or not?"

"Nooo," she moaned.

"She's hurt!" Taylor yanked the door open. Water rushed in, soaking the already wet carpeting.

"I'm not waiting. You two are on your own. Have fun explaining why you stole a car." Luke laughed and loped off up the boat ramp, disappearing into the shadows.

Taylor swore under his breath and pulled Marissa around so he could see her face in the moonlight.

"Ooow." She cried and doubled over. Her bloody face and hands looked ghoulish in the moonlight.

Taylor pried her hands away and dunked them in the water. "Splash a little water on your face to wash the blood off." He waited then encouraged her to wipe it off with her t-shirt. The moonlight exposed on a gash in her forehead.

Voices from somewhere on the hill above them drew their attention. Two lights bobbed toward them. Taylor pulled Marissa from the car. "You gotta get out of here."

"I can't. My head hurts." She whined and stumbled into him.

Taylor grabbed her by the shoulders and pressed the tip of his nose to hers. "You don't have a choice. Dad will kill you if he finds out about this. Now go!" He stepped aside and pushed her toward the shore. "Stay in the shadows and go back the way you did the other night. Don't make any noise."

Marissa looked back at him, one hand clutching her forehead. Moonlit tears glistened on her cheeks. She sniffed. "Taybo, the car. I'm so sorry." Another sob escaped Marissa's lips.

"Shhh! Get out of here. Hurry!"

Marissa staggered into the shadow of the tree where Taylor'd been caught two nights before and he turned his attention to the car. He had to get it out of the water. Maybe Paul and his God Squad buddy would help him push it back up onto shore. Footsteps pounded down the steps to the boathouse. Flashlight beams jumped crazily across the water, catching Taylor in their glare. He couldn't see a thing, but he knew the voice.

"You again?" Paul aimed his flashlight full in Taylor's face. "Didn't you "

"Hey." His buddy interrupted him. "Isn't that Roberto's Mustang?" His flashlight played over the car.

Taylor shaded his eyes with his hands. "Yeah, it's Roberto's. Cut the light and help me get it out of the water."

Paul's flashlight splayed across the car. "Oh, man, he's gonna freak."

"C'mon, help me push it out." Taylor waded around to the front and lowered his shoulder against the damaged front end. He threw all his weight against it, but the car barely moved. Paul and the other guy kicked off their shoes and waded into the water.

Playing his flashlight around the interior, Paul asked, "How'd you get the keys?"

"Roberto left them with me." Taylor pushed against the car again.

"Yeah, right." Paul reached inside the car. "Hang on. Let me put it in neutral." He shifted, then closed the door and got into position to push from the side. His buddy moved to the front with Taylor. "You guys ready? On three. One, two, three."

The car crept backward until all four tires rested on dry ground. Paul reached in and pushed the gearshift to park.

Easing up and away from the car, Taylor expelled a breath. No telling how much damage the water had already done to the engine. He winced as the moonlight accented the dents and scratches from the gate. A flashlight beam hit him in the eyes again.

"Now, you want to tell me how you got the keys, and why you took Roberto's car for a joyride?"

TAYLOR FOCUSED on a knot in the wood floor beside Zeke's desk and refused to answer the second question. Fingering Luke meant bringing Marissa into the blame as well, and he couldn't let that happen. Even with Roberto thinking the worst of him. Even with Zeke calling the police.

How many hours had passed since Paul called Zeke? Taylor rubbed his eyes. They felt grainy and sore and he desperately wanted to close them, to sleep. Maybe when he woke up, this nightmare would end.

Despite the early morning hour, Zeke had called Roberto. The older man shuffled into the office and sank onto the other chair in front of Zeke's desk. Roberto's unshaven face lacked its customary cheerfulness. Droopy eyes, knitted brow and a serious frown replaced his elation from the previous evening. He balanced on the edge of the chair, shoulders rounded, hands clasped between his knees. Yes, he'd left in a hurry and forgot the keys, but trusted Taylor to keep them until the next day.

Taylor kept his face averted. He couldn't stand to see the hurt and betrayal he expected in Roberto's eyes.

You dirt bag, Luke. You beat me. With Marissa involved, Luke knew he was safe. He knew Taylor would never allow her to be linked with trouble.

Zeke took off his reading glasses and pinched the bridge of his nose. He leaned back in his chair and spoke to Roberto. "I've asked the boys to tow the car back up to the shed as soon as it's light enough. You can look it over and decide what needs to be done. I'm so sorry, Roberto. I could've prevented this."

Roberto's protest was cut short by the phone. Zeke answered it, gave a quick okay and hung up. "Deputy Scott is on his way."

Dad was right. I'm going to jail, just like Jesse. Except I didn't do anything wrong!

Roberto's chair creaked as he shifted his weight. "I do no' want to press charges."

Taylor lifted his head. For the first time, he dared to look at Roberto. He'd never seen the man in anything other than his tan work uniform, but here he sat in jean shorts and a white t-shirt.

"Are you certain?" Zeke asked. "Stealing a car, even on private property, is a serious matter."

Roberto straightened, throwing his shoulders back, and planted his hands firmly on his knees. "No. No charges."

"You've put a tremendous amount of money and work into that car, Roberto." Zeke leaned forward, elbows on his desk. "I admire what you tried to do here with Taylor, but he needs to understand the seriousness of his actions."

"He did not drive the car into the water."

"He was caught red-handed," Zeke argued. "There was no one else around when the boys found him. He was trying to get the car out of the lake by himself."

Roberto turned his head, meeting Taylor's gaze. His voice was quiet but firm. "I do not believe it."

Taylor's pulse thundered in his ears. Roberto's eyes held no hint of doubt or condemnation. Unable to breathe, he stared at the floor again. All the evidence pointed to him. How could Roberto not believe it? What if they discovered the truth? What if Marissa got in trouble after all? He couldn't let that happen, even if he ended up in jail. *Better me than her.*

"I did it." Taylor blurted it out. Both men regarded him in stunned silence. He faced Roberto, shaking his head. "I'm sorry. I am really sorry. I wasn't trying to steal it. I just—I couldn't wait to see how it felt to drive it."

Roberto said nothing. A shadow clouded his eyes and he exchanged glances with Zeke.

Taylor pressed his lips together to stop the quivering, and

blinked hard against the moisture gathering in his eyes. Keeping Marissa out of trouble meant betraying the kindest man he'd ever met. *Why did it have to be this way?* He closed his eyes and covered his face with his hands.

Roberto stood, his steps heavy as he came close and squeezed Taylor's shoulder before shuffling out the door. It wasn't a vise grip, like Dad would've given him, but a firm, gentle squeeze that communicated what? Not anger. Grief, maybe, but more like encouragement, forgivenesslike Brady's comment at lunch. Forgiveness? After he'd confessed to stealing the car and driving it into the lake?

Taylor's gut tightened like a spring about to snap. Doubled over, nauseous, he clenched his teeth and pictured every single one of his dreams crashing into the lake and sinking, just like Roberto's Mustang.

Z eke's chair squeaked and his hands came to rest on Taylor's shoulders. *Was he praying?* It didn't matter. Nothing would help now. He might as well get used to the idea of going to jail—not finishing school, not getting his driver's license, not seeing his friends or Marissa or his family for a long time. He breathed deep, fighting back the wetness at the corners of his eyes.

Zeke prayed the Lord's Prayer aloud. "Forgive us our trespasses, as we forgive those who trespass against us. And lead us not into temptation, but deliver us from evil. For thine is the kingdom, the power and the glory forever and ever. Amen."

Taylor straightened and drew in a shuddering breath as he dragged his fingers down his face to get rid of any telltale moisture. Someone rang the bell to wake up the campers. If only he could wake up too, but the nightmare continued.

A sheriff's deputy in a brown uniform rapped on the door of Zeke's office.

"Morning, Zeke. Kind of early in the day for problems, isn't it?" He assumed a wide-legged stance, hooking his thumbs into the front of his belt. His head tipped sideways to observe Taylor.

Zeke rose to his feet, but kept one hand on Taylor's shoulder. "I'm afraid so. Deputy Scott, this is Taylor Dixon. It seems he went for a joy ride last night in a car that belongs to my facilities manager—a 1970 Mustang he's been restoring. A couple of my security guys found Taylor with the car down at the lake, in the water."

Deputy Scott moved closer and half sat on the edge of Zeke's desk. "How old are you, Taylor?"

"Fifteen."

"Are you in driver's ed?" Taylor shook his head, keeping his eyes averted.

The officer folded his arms across his chest. "What made you decide to take the car?"

Taylor gave a tiny shrug.

Zeke's voice was gentle, prodding. "Go ahead and tell him, son. You've got nothing to lose."

Taylor swallowed hard. "I wasn't stealing it."

"Why'd you drive it into the lake?"

"I didn't mean to drive it into the lake. It wouldn't stop. The brakes aren't connected."

"You didn't know about the brakes?" Zeke asked.

"No. Roberto kept saying it wasn't ready to drive yet, but he never mentioned the brakes."

Deputy Scott took a notepad out of his shirt pocket. "And you did this all by yourself? Not to show off to a friend or a girl maybe?"

Taylor shook his head.

The officer addressed Zeke. "I'll need to talk with Roberto. Is he around?"

"He was here, but he left. He doesn't want to press charges."

"Well, if he doesn't want to pursue it, there's not much I can do since it was on private property."

"What do you suggest then?"

Officer Scott stood. "Let's all take a walk out to my patrol car. I want to show Taylor something."

Taylor pushed himself to his feet. His legs shook, threatening to collapse as he followed the officer out the door. Zeke trailed behind them. The squad car was parked in front of the Snack Shack, where everyone would see it on the way to breakfast. A few early birds had already stopped to check their Rec assignments. They hurried out of the way as soon as they saw Taylor with the deputy, but took their time getting to the dining hall, casting curious looks over their shoulders every few steps.

Mechanical voices chattered on the car's radio when Deputy Scott opened the rear door.

"Take a look, Taylor," he said. "This is where you'll be sitting if Roberto changes his mind."

Facing the car, Taylor shut his eyes, but he couldn't keep out images of what lay ahead for him, nor the memories of Jesse being put into a patrol car. He opened his eyes and looked inside, noticing the steel reinforcements on the back of the front seats. The clear protective shield between the officer in front and the prisoner in back. No handle on the door and no window control meant no escape. Taylor drew his shoulders in close, crossing his arms tight across his chest. How long would they make him stand here staring at this portable prison cell?

A familiar laugh cackled in the morning quiet. From the corner of his eye, Taylor saw Luke approaching with another kid from the cabin.

"Oh, look! Someone's in trouble." Luke's sing-songy voice sparked heat in Taylor's cheeks. Zeke urged Luke on his way while Deputy Scott took Taylor by the arm and guided him into the back seat of the patrol car. The seat was hard, some type of uncomfortable molded plastic. There was barely enough room for his legs, and the ceiling was low, giving the back seat a cramped feel. Would they handcuff him, too?

A scream split the air. "Taybo! No! No! You can't arrest him.

He didn't do it." Marissa tore away from Claire's side to push between Zeke and Deputy Scott.

Taylor jumped from the car. He grabbed Marissa by the shoulders, barely noticing the angry gash on her forehead, and spoke through clenched teeth. "Shut up, Rissa! Shut up. Don't say anything."

Marissa ignored him, turning her head and reaching for the officer. "You can't arrest him." She twisted out of Taylor's grip and grabbed the deputy's arm. "He didn't do anything. It was my fault. Please don't arrest him."

Taylor went after her. "She's lying. Don't listen to her. Marissa, shut up!"

Zeke took Marissa's hands in his while Officer Scott restrained Taylor. Claire watched in open-mouthed silence.

"Calm down," Zeke ordered. "No one is arresting Taylor. At least, not yet."

Marissa struggled to free herself from Zeke's grasp, still pleading with Deputy Scott. "You can't arrest him. He didn't take the car. Taylor would never do that." Tears streamed down her cheeks and dripped from her chin. Hair clung to her wet cheeks and she used her shoulder to brush it away. "Please! Let Taylor go. He didn't do it."

"Marissa." Zeke's calm voice brought her attention back to him. "Do you know who took the car?"

"Yes, it was Luke. Taylor had nothing to do with it."

16

M arissa's pleas drew the attention of more campers on their way to breakfast. Zeke assured her that Taylor wasn't being arrested.

"But I think we need to sort this out in my office." He released Marissa, turned and nearly bumped into Claire. "You're not part of this, too, are you?"

Claire's head moved side to side, her eyes as big as Rustic Knoll's dinner plates.

"She helped me last night," Marissa pointed to her forehead, "helped me clean up the blood after I got back to the cabin."

Zeke took a good look at her wound. "What happened?"

"I hit my head when the car went into the lake." Marissa reached out and clung to Claire's arm. "We were going to see Nurse Willie when I saw Taylor there in the car."

"All right, Claire, you'd better come too." Zeke led the way to his office.

Taylor pulled away from the officer. Anything he said would be overheard by Zeke and the deputy, so Taylor hurried to Marissa's side and shot her a warning glance. One arm still linked with Claire's, Marissa slipped her other arm through his. Did she misunderstand? Or was she trying to suck up to him? Taylor jerked away and put some distance between them.

The five of them crowded into Zeke's office. Taylor and Marissa took the two armchairs and Zeke offered Claire his own padded desk chair. Officer Scott closed the door. Zeke stood at his desk. "Now, tell me what happened last night."

Marissa sniffed. "Taylor didn't do anything wrong." She glanced sideways at Taylor, then kept her eyes downcast. Her hands and fingers twisted in her lap and her chin quivered. She sniffed again. "It was Luke who took the car out. He told me to meet him at the garage at midnight. Said we'd go for a ride in the Mustang."

Zeke interrupted. "How did Luke get the key?"

Marissa shrugged and looked at Taylor. All eyes fastened on him.

"Taylor," Zeke asked, "do you know how Luke got the key?"

Taylor sat on his hands. Everything was falling apart. He might as well tell the truth. At least he wouldn't be going to jail, but Dad's reaction to this whole mess might make him wish for a jail cell.

"I had Roberto's keys in my shorts pocket. Luke must've taken them while I was sleeping."

"You had the keys because Roberto left quickly and asked you to close up, right? How did Luke know about the key and where you put it?" Zeke half-sat on his desk.

"He showed up at the garage last night after Roberto left. I was closing up. I'm sure he saw me put them in my pocket. He tried to get me to take the car out then, but I told him it wasn't ready yet."

Zeke's forefinger brushed his mustache as he switched his gaze to Marissa. "What happened when you met Luke?"

"He was waiting for me and he had a key that unlocked the side door. He showed me the button that opens the garage door and told me to open it as soon as he got the car started. It took him a few tries, but when he got it running, I opened the door and we took off." Marissa shivered and wrapped her arms around her waist. "He floored it right away, and we were going so fast. We almost hit a tree. I screamed for him to slow down, but he yelled at me that the brakes weren't working. I think he made it slow down a little with the gear shift, but he needed both hands just to steer, to keep it on the road."

Marissa's face scrunched up and tears squeezed from beneath her closed eyelids. Her hands flew up to cover her mouth and her voice rose to a tiny, bird-like pitch. "I was so scared. We hit that gate and then all of a sudden, we were in the water. I thought I was going to die. I'm so sorry." She clutched her middle and bent over, burying her face in her knees. Her shoulders shook.

Claire slipped from her seat and knelt beside Marissa. Her arms encircled the sobbing girl.

Zeke's eyes shifted to Taylor. "Is this the truth?"

Taylor pressed his lips together and nodded. "I think so. As far as I know." He glanced up long enough to see Zeke's serious expression soften.

"Why did you tell Roberto you took the car?"

"So Marissa wouldn't get caught. If I told on Luke, I knew he'd say Marissa was with him. I couldn't let her get in trouble."

The director's white eyebrows drew together. "Why not?"

"Because I'm responsible for her."

"Who made you responsible for Marissa?"

"Mom and Dad." Taylor shrugged. "I've always had to watch out for her."

Zeke frowned. "And you'd take the blame for stealing a car rather than let her get caught?"

Taylor frowned and nodded, bringing on a fresh flood of tears from Marissa. Zeke offered Marissa a box of tissues. Claire sat on the floor at Marissa's feet, holding her hand.

Zeke and Deputy Scott exchanged looks, then Zeke asked, "Marissa, if we question Luke and he says something different "

"If he says something different, he's lying." Marissa sat up straight and took a deep breath. She looked at Taylor. "I should've listened to you. Both times, he left me alone and let you take the blame." She dabbed her eyes, then blew her nose.

Zeke held up his hand. "Wait. Both times?"

Marissa hung her head. "I met Luke down at the lake Tuesday night. Taylor showed up and told me to go back to the cabin."

The white eyebrows reached high on his forehead. "And Taylor took the blame for that, too." Zeke continued rubbing his mustache as he looked from Marissa to Taylor. "Come with me. Let's go see if we can find Luke." He waited for everyone to stand, then led the way to the dining hall.

Upon entering the hall, Taylor's gaze swept across the spacious room, searching the campers at each table.

Marissa stood beside him on tiptoes and pointed to a table near the center of the room. "That's him in the blue t-shirt with his back to us."

Zeke instructed everyone to wait there while he went to talk with Luke. He weaved around the breakfast tables and leaned down to speak into Luke's ear.

Luke nodded and stood up. He picked up his tray, but set it back on the table when Zeke said something. He started toward the dining room exit, but as soon as he caught sight of Taylor and Marissa, he slowed almost to a stop. From behind, Zeke urged him forward and almost instantly, his narrowed eyes opened wide and his lips relaxed into a lazy smile. He walked up to Deputy Scott and extended his hand. "Good morning, Officer."

Zeke kept his hand on Luke's shoulder while giving instructions to Taylor and the girls. "You kids get some breakfast while we talk to Luke. Claire, you can go on to Bible study when you're finished. Taylor and Marissa, wait for me here."

The buzz of conversation in the dining hall intensified as Zeke and Deputy Scott escorted Luke out the door. Taylor exhaled, the tension in his shoulders easing away in a slow melt.

He and Marissa and Claire said little as they made their way through the buffet line. Nothing looked appetizing. The events of the last several hours had left his stomach as unsettled as his brain. And what if Janie came out of the kitchen? Did she know about the car yet? He grabbed a couple individual boxes of cereal and a carton of milk and hustled away from the serving line.

Marissa and Claire sat at a table well away from anyone else, and Taylor joined them, his back to the rest of the room. The last thing he wanted was to answer questions from Nick or any of the other kids who might have seen him sitting in the cop car. He emptied the cereal into a bowl, poured milk on it and put a spoonful in his mouth. It tasted like cardboard. Maybe it would go down easier if he poured more milk on it.

Marissa and Claire huddled close, both totally focused on their plates though they didn't seem to be eating much either. No one spoke until Claire stood up, mumbled "See you later," and left the table.

Marissa toyed with the last few bites of her French toast and eggs. "What'll happen to me, Taybo? Do you think I'll go to jail?"

Taylor shrugged and lifted one eyebrow. "Who knows?" He gave up on the cereal and pushed the bowl away. "Why'd you do it?"

Marissa frowned and pushed little pieces of French toast around her plate with her fork. "I really wanted Luke to like me."

"I know that. But why'd you tell? You shouldn't have said anything. They didn't know a thing about you and Luke."

Marissa gave him that look, like he was the dumbest thing alive. "They were going to arrest you. It's bad enough Jesse's in prison. How could I let you go to jail for something I did? I'd never be able to live with that." She shoved her tray aside, crossed her arms on the table and hid her face in them.

The sniffles told him she was crying again. She'd finally owned up to doing something stupid, but Taylor's mouth went dry imagining Dad's reaction. He'd never get his license now.

The dining hall had cleared out by the time Zeke walked in. Marissa raised her head as he pulled up a chair and laid his hands flat on the table, fingers splayed with thumbs touching. "Luke admitted taking the car, but he won't say anything else. During the day when he's not in session, he'll be confined to my office. Harris is with him now, gathering some things from the cabin. I'll be calling both his and your parents and asking them to meet with me tomorrow when they come to pick you up." Zeke slid one hand in Marissa's direction. "You understand what you and Luke did was wrong?"

She sniffed and nodded.

"Not only wrong, but dangerous and foolish as well."

"I know." The last word trailed off into more tears. "I'm so sorry. What's going to happen to me?"

"You're fortunate Roberto still refuses to press charges, but I'll be asking Luke's and your parents to share the cost of repairs to the car."

Taylor's stomach sank. He let go his last hope of getting out of this without Dad finding out.

Zeke continued talking to Marissa. "You'll need to apologize to Roberto. And I'd like to talk with you some more, but we'll wait until this afternoon." He slid his other hand toward Taylor. "I've told Roberto how everything happened. He said he knew all along you didn't take the car. And, I owe you an apology. I was quick to judge you guilty based on our previous encounters. I'm sorry, Taylor, and I beg your forgiveness."

Taylor straightened. Zeke apologizing to him? Asking his forgiveness?

"Um, sure. No problem."

"There's something I want both of you to understand. Whatever your family agreement has been in the past, Marissa, you're old enough now to know right from wrong. It's time for you to start making wise decisions. And Taylor, the more you cover up for your sister, the longer it will take her to learn that poor choices have ugly consequences. I admire your willingness to protect her, but part of growing up is learning to accept the results of our actions. Give your sister some room and let her grow into the beautiful and responsible young lady she was meant to be." He looked from one to the other. "Understood?"

Taylor nodded. *Tell that to Dad when you ask him to help pay for the car.*

"Okay, then." Zeke pushed back his chair and stood up. "Go put your dishes away and head on to Bible study. Marissa, come see me at lunch time and we'll go talk to Roberto."

Taylor put his tray on the conveyor belt behind Marissa's and followed her outside.

"Are you going back to get your Bible?" she asked.

"No, I'm going to find Roberto."

"But Zeke just told us to go to Bible study."

Taylor ignored her and kept walking toward the garage.

"Taybo, didn't you just hear what Zeke said about making wise decisions?"

"Yeah." He faced her, walking backward. "He said that to you. I need to ask Roberto something." He left Marissa and jogged off toward the garage. Had they towed the car back yet? He'd seen the damage under last night's full moon. How much worse would it be in daylight?

Taylor halted at the edge of the parking lot. All the bay doors were closed, the camp pickup truck gone. Where was Roberto? He needed to find him, needed the answer to one question.

Why did he believe in me when everything and everyone said I was guilty?

17

A chugging sound grew louder and Taylor peered down the service road. The Rustic Knoll pickup topped the rise and turned into the parking lot. Roberto's elbow hung out the driver's side window. Paul and his buddy rode in the back, keeping watch over the Mustang in tow. Roberto circled in front of the garage, positioning the Mustang to slip back into its bay. The guys jumped down from the back, opened the garage door and directed Roberto as he backed the Mustang into the garage. Taylor ran up while they were unhitching it.

Paul stopped and glared at him. "What are you doing here? Didn't you see enough last night?"

Roberto shushed him. "He did not do this."

"Yeah, right." Paul took a step toward Taylor, but Roberto blocked his way.

"Finish what you are doing." Roberto stood beside Taylor while Paul returned to freeing the car from the back of the truck.

Seeing the damage in daylight brought a lump to Taylor's throat that made it difficult to talk. Dents and scratches marred the hood. The flattened chrome bumper had taken the brunt of the gate's bottom crossbar. The grille was smashed and one headlamp shattered. Who knew how bad the engine might be after sitting in water?

As soon as the car was unhitched, the guys drove off in the pickup. Taylor swallowed hard, unable to take his eyes off the car. "I'm so, so sorry."

Roberto twisted his head to look at Taylor. "Why do you apologize? Is not your fault."

"Yes, it is." Taylor shoved his hands deep into his pockets. "I should've left when you did last night, but I stayed around, sat in the car and turned it on. If I'd left, Luke wouldn't have found me here. He wouldn't have known I had the key. Or maybe I should've given the key to Zeke instead of waiting to give it to you." He couldn't meet the older man's gaze.

Roberto moved to stand in front of Taylor. "You did nothing wrong. He took the key from your pocket. He is the one who drove the car to the lake."

Taylor raised his eyes to Roberto's. "Why were you so sure it wasn't me? You knew I wanted to try out the car. All the evidence pointed to me, but you didn't believe it. How did you know I didn't take it?"

A smile creased Roberto's face. "Because I see what is here." His calloused forefinger pointed at Taylor's chest near his heart. "You love car too much to do this."

"But how?" Taylor asked. "How did you know?"

Roberto shuffled over to the Mustang, lifted the damaged hood and propped it open, then moved aside and beckoned Taylor to join him. Leaning his bronze forearms on the left fender, he pointed to the engine.

"You remember the pictures?" He jerked his thumb at the photo album above the workbench. "The first ones?"

Taylor nodded. Those first pictures, taken shortly after Roberto bought the car, showed a filthy engine. A mouse had even built a nest in it.

Roberto pointed to the engine again. "Is same engine as in

pictures. I take apart, clean, rebuild. Now, is like new." He pointed to his chest. "Same with my heart. Your heart. We get dirty, plugged up. But God—He take our heart, sometimes He break it apart, clean it, restore it. Just like engine." His gaze roamed over the car. "You and car both need repair, restore. Si?"

Taylor turned that over in his mind. With a car and an engine, that made sense, but was it really the same with people? "How does that explain—I mean, I lied to your face. Even when I said I wrecked the car, you didn't believe me. Why?"

Roberto chewed his lip a moment then asked, "Why you say you take it?"

Taylor raked his hair back from his face. He paced to the workbench. "If I had ratted on Luke, he would've told everyone Marissa was with him. I couldn't let her get in trouble."

"Why not?"

Why not? Hadn't he told her he wouldn't bail her out anymore? Was he so used to protecting her, like a habit he couldn't break? No, his reason was much more serious. If he lost Marissa, he'd have no one to believe in his dreams. Could he admit to that?

Taylor shrugged. "I've always watched out for her, ever since I can remember."

"And you would go to jail for her?"

Taylor inhaled a shaky breath. That was a close call, but yes, he'd have gone to jail in her place.

Roberto's hand gripped his shoulder, turning him so they stood face to face. "Your sister too is like dirty engine, no? Always giving trouble?"

Taylor's mouth pulled up on one side, imagining Marissa's reaction to being called a dirty engine, but Roberto got the trouble part right.

"And you would take punishment for her. You would go to prison so she does not have to, si?"

Taylor nodded, still trying to figure out where this was going.

"You would do for her what Jesus did for us, for you. Not prison, but a cross." He tapped his fingers against Taylor's chest. "Is good heart in there, like good engine, but needs work—cleaning, rebuilding to make like new. Restore. Ask Jesus to clean it, make it new. He is waiting for you to ask."

Now the pieces were fitting together. Taylor recalled Zeke's words from last night. He hadn't paid close attention, but he did remember Zeke reading a Psalm, one that King David had written after his affair with Bathsheba and the arranged murder of her husband. Pretty bad stuff compared to what Taylor had done. But David asked God to forgive him, to wash his heart and make it clean, to restore his heart.

Roberto looked him square in the eye. "Comprende?"

"Yeah, I understand what you're saying, but how does it happen? I mean, how does Jesus do that—restore a heart?"

Roberto dropped his hand from Taylor's shoulder and shrugged. "Is a mystery. You ask. Find out." He turned back to the car and opened the door. Leaning in, he pressed his hand into the carpet. Water squished up between his fingers.

Taylor followed him, peeking over his shoulder. "Will you have to replace all that new carpet?"

Roberto pursed his lips. "Maybe not, if I take out, clean and lay in sun to dry."

"I'll help. The sooner we take the seats out, the sooner we can pull that carpet out and get it drying."

Roberto checked his watch. "You are supposed to be in Bible study, no?"

Taylor shrugged. "It's kind of late to join my group. Besides, it's the last day and I just had the best lesson of the week from you."

Roberto chuckled. "One time, Zeke will not mind. Let's work."

～

THE BELL WAS CALLING campers to lunch by the time Taylor and Roberto finished pulling out the carpet and laying it out in the sun to dry. Nick was at the cabin when Taylor ran back to change the clothes he'd been wearing since late last night. Actually, he'd worn them most of yesterday, too. No wonder they'd developed their own fragrance.

Nick barely took a breath when he saw Taylor. "Where've you been? Why were you sitting in that sheriff's car? Someone said that old guy's Mustang was in the lake. Did you take it? I couldn't believe you'd do something like that. What's going on?"

Taylor filled Nick in on everything while he threw on a different t-shirt and shorts. Sliding his feet into flip-flops, he rubbed his growling stomach. "Come on, let's go eat."

As they neared the dining hall, the spot where the police car had been parked stirred all the emotions from the long night. Everything from anger and fear to hope and gratitude. He wouldn't face Dad's wrath for stealing a car, but what about Dad's reaction when he found out Marissa was involved? Taylor shuddered and set the thought aside. He'd worry about that later. Right now, he had to get through lunch and all the curious stares from the other campers. He never wanted to see the back seat of a police car again. Ever.

WHOSE IDEA WAS it to smear lard all over a watermelon, throw it in the lake and make forty or more campers try to hold onto it long enough to lift it onto the pier?

Taylor's hands clamped around the sides of the slippery oversized football, but it squirted away. He let it go and watched the others chase it. Chasing a greased watermelon around the swimming area was stupid. The whole water carnival seemed pointless compared to thinking he was going to jail for something he didn't do, then being found not guilty. Or maybe he was just tired after being up all night.

Now and then, he caught a glimpse of Claire in the middle of the action, but Taylor stayed on the edge of the crowd, following the massive jumble of shrieking campers from one side of the shallow swim area to the other. Both teams fought to move the watermelon toward their goal, while the lifeguard paced back and forth on the pier, whistle clamped between his teeth.

At last, the other team hoisted the watermelon onto the pier, and the lifeguard blew a blast on his whistle. Claire waded out of the water, holding up her greasy hands and grimacing at the slippery mess on her swimsuit. "Gross!" She shook the sand from her towel before wiping her hands on it and wrapping it around her waist.

Taylor slung his towel around his neck and they walked up to the grassy hill above the beach.

Claire shaded her eyes from the bright afternoon sun. "I was looking for you earlier. Wanted you to do the canoe race with me, but I couldn't find you."

Taylor had turned around to watch the lake, but snapped his focus back to Claire. "Seriously? You wanted me in your canoe after what I did to you last year?"

"Sure!" Her cheeks dimpled as she smiled. "I figured you wouldn't dump me out if we were both in the same canoe."

Taylor smiled then fastened his gaze on the lake before him. The water sparkled in the afternoon sunshine, but he didn't really see it. Instead, his mind bounced from image to image—the car nose-deep in the lake, the back seat of the police car and Marissa's tearful confession, the engine as a picture of his heart. And over it all hung Zeke's question. *What's in your heart?* It was just like Roberto said. His heart was like a dirty, old, plugged up engine that needed cleaning and restoring. He turned to Claire. "I'm sorry about last year."

Claire studied him for several moments before she spoke.

"Okay, I've been trying to decide if you've changed since last year or if I just understand you a little better after knowing Marissa."

Taylor tugged on the ends of his towel. "And? What'd you decide?"

"After what I heard this morning, I think there's a pretty cool guy hiding in there somewhere. You should let him out more often."

18

A fraid of falling asleep before the final campfire was over, Taylor searched for someone to sit with. He scanned the circular rows of campers, their faces lit by the fire's dancing orange glow. No use sitting next to Nick. With camp ending tomorrow, his buddy would be so focused on Alex, he probably wouldn't even know Taylor was there. Who else could he sit with? Claire? Nope, not with Marissa beside her. In a section across from them, Taylor spotted some room near Steven and Brady. He slid in next to Brady. "Hey, nice job at the talent show."

"What?" Brady's voice held disbelief.

Steven leaned forward and spoke across Brady. "I thought you weren't impressed with trumpet solos."

"That was last year." Taylor glanced at Brady. "This year is different."

The corners of Brady's mouth curved up. "Thanks. I heard about Luke and the car. Good thing your sister bailed you out." A couple counselors strummed their guitars and Brady turned his attention to the music.

Was it a good thing Marissa bailed him out? Not going to jail was a good thing, but they still had to face Dad tomorrow. He tugged his sweaty shirt away from his back. The air was already warm, too warm for a campfire. Moisture in the burning wood hissed and crackled. The flames licked higher, sending a narrow plume of smoke up into the night sky. The odor of bug spray overwhelmed the smoky smell, with little air circulation where he sat in the middle of this crowd of campers.

Running lights from a motorboat crossed the lake, its low hum audible only during a break in the music. Taylor's gaze followed a spark drifting away from the fire until it burned out then reignited. *Not a spark but a lightning bug.* Harris, along with Luke, squeezed in next to him and Taylor scooted closer to Brady. Taylor hunched his shoulders together, even more uncomfortable than before.

Harris leaned toward him. "Zeke filled me in on what happened. I guess I owe you an apology. I worked you hard that one morning for making me lose sleep. Forgive me. I'm sorry about the car, too."

Taylor shrugged. "It's okay." Would it have made any difference if he'd told Harris the truth? Doubt it, but it was nice to hear him admit he was wrong.

The guitars continued playing softly in the background while a counselor stood up to speak. "All week, Zeke has been asking what's in your heart. Have you answered that question? Have you found any of the stuff he's talked about—jealousy, selfishness, foul language?" He held up his Bible. "It says here all of us have sinned and fallen short of what God requires. Every last one of us, and it's impossible to please God that way. But the cool thing about God is that He still loves us, even in our filth and our greed and when we only think about ourselves. He loves us too much to make us suffer the punishment we deserve. That's why He sent Jesus, His own son, to take our punishment. When we believe that, when we trust that He loved us enough to do that, God doesn't see the mess anymore when He looks at our heart.

He sees Jesus on the cross and says, 'My child, you are forgiven.' We may still feel guilty, but Romans 8:1-2 says there is no condemnation for those who trust in Jesus' sacrifice, because He has set us free from the law that requires punishment for our sin."

That's what Roberto was saying this morning. Hard to believe, after all the stuff he'd done to Luke, Brady and the others—after all the mean things he'd said—God could still love him. Dad's unending criticism and punishment made it hard to imagine the kind of God Roberto and Zeke and the others talked about. Dad probably loved him. Didn't he? He never hesitated to punish Taylor when it looked like he'd done something wrong. Or when Marissa did something wrong.

Brady elbowed him. "Hey, isn't that your sister?"

Marissa? *Why is she standing up?* Taylor mentally backtracked. He hadn't been paying attention, but he'd heard enough to recall the counselor's request for personal stories. *Oh, no.*

Marissa's small but determined voice rang out in the darkness, her face lit by the campfire's ever changing flames. "This is my first year at camp, but it has made a huge change in my life. I've been pretty much all about myself, doing what I wanted to do no matter how it affected other people. I like having fun, especially if it's something a little daring. But this week, I saw what that was doing to me and to—someone I love." She sniffed and wiped her eyes. A smile flitted across her face as she glanced Taylor's way. "Don't worry, I won't embarrass you."

Taylor ducked behind the kid sitting in front of him.

"I made some really stupid choices and," Marissa's voice rose and quivered, "I expected someone else to take the punishment for me, because that's how it's always worked. But this week, I saw how selfish I've been and how much that hurts people I love. So from now on, I'm going to make better choices. Jesus already took my punishment, just like my bro I mean, someone else always did. I'm believing what the Bible says so I can become someone new." Marissa sat down. She received an immediate hug from Claire and applause from the rest of the campers.

Taylor waited until someone else stood before he dared sit up straight. Brady and Harris both nudged him and nodded their approval, while Luke sat stone-faced.

Marissa got it. She understood what Roberto was telling him this morning, what Zeke and the counselors had been saying all week. Envy over her quick understanding pricked Taylor's chest like the mosquito on his foot. He stomped and reached down to scratch the itch. Roberto's words came back to him. *You would do for her what Jesus did for you.*

Taylor lifted his eyes to the lake beyond the campfire. Lights twinkled along the opposite shore, bigger and brighter than the thousands of stars overhead. He blocked out the campfire, the kid speaking, Brady and Harris on either side of him and stared at the lights and the stars above them.

God, I don't know how this works, but I know what I was willing to do to keep Rissa out of trouble. And if I'd do that for her, I guess maybe you'd do the same for me. I hope you love me like everyone says, because I'm as messed up as Roberto's old engine. Right now, I'm asking you to clean out my heart, or my gut, or my life. Whatever. I was expecting the worst punishment, but Roberto believed in me and Rissa cared enough about me to save me from that punishment. So, I'm going to believe in Jesus and trust You to do what the Bible says you'll do.

Taylor drew in a long breath and let it out slowly. Now what? Was something supposed to happen—lightning or angels singing or something? Shouldn't he feel different? The campfire burned a little lower. The counselor strummed the guitar a little slower and the campers sang a soft, meditative song. Hmm, maybe something was different. He didn't feel cramped anymore, even though he was still scrunched in between Brady and Steven on one side and Harris and Luke on the other.

Taylor looked up again into the sky. Free. That's how he felt, like a part of him could soar up there with the stars. All this time, he'd been living in a prison, but it wasn't the same as Jesse's prison. No, he'd built this one for himself out of jealousy, anger and resentment. But God freed him, in spite of all that. It was a mystery, like Roberto said. God wasn't waiting to punish or condemn him. He felt as free as when he'd imagined himself driving the Mustang out on the open road.

Free. The word ran through his head the rest of the evening, and all the way back to the cabin. He barely heard Harris's devotions, the way it kept echoing in his thoughts. After brushing his teeth, Taylor went back to the bunkroom and pulled back the top of his sleeping bag. He wouldn't need it tonight, not with the warmth of the evening.

Two bunks over, Luke stood beside his bed. He'd pulled back his sleeping bag, too. Completely unzipped and opened all the way. From where he stood, Taylor could see a couple smears of squished night crawlers on the inside of the bag. Taylor grabbed his own bag off his bed and padded over to Luke's bunk. "Here, you can use mine if you need it tonight."

Luke's eyes narrowed. His lip curled into an ugly sneer. "I don't need anything from you." He closed his sleeping bag and lay down on top of it, his back to Taylor.

Hands tight around his sleeping bag, Taylor marched back to his bunk. *The jerk won't even accept a peace offering.* A hand touched his back and he turned to find Steven behind him.

"Nice try," Steven said, his voice low, "even if he didn't take it."

"Yeah, thanks." Taylor took a deep breath and dropped the bag onto his bed. Habits are hard to break, but he wasn't going to allow the old anger and resentment to imprison him again. He was free.

"CAN you hear what they're saying in there?" Marissa gave up her perch on her suitcase and slid to the floor in the hall outside Zeke's office.

Taylor shook his head but inched closer to Zeke's closed door. He recognized each voice coming from inside the office—Dad, Luke's dad, Roberto and Zeke—but he couldn't tell what they were saying. Luke was in there, too, but he'd been mostly silent. Claire appeared at the other end of the hallway.

"There you are! I've been looking all over for you to say good-bye."

Marissa jumped to her feet and hugged Claire's neck. "Thank you so-o-o much for everything this week. Things would've turned out a lot different if you hadn't been in my cabin, looking out for me."

Claire returned the hug, throwing Taylor a dimpled smile over Marissa's shoulder. "We had some fun, didn't we? You're coming back next year, right?" She released the hug, but still held onto Marissa's arms. "And you've got my cell number so be sure to let me know how things go."

"I will." Marissa gave her a firm squeeze before letting go. "And I'll see you next year."

Claire wiggled her fingers at Taylor. "See you next year, too. Bye!"

Taylor waved. Maybe if he'd stood up, she'd have hugged him, too. Or not. At least she was talking to him, instead of turning her back like she did on Sunday.

Marissa settled back onto the floor. "How long are they going to talk?" She sighed and rested her elbow on her knee, head in hand.

Moments later, the door opened. Luke's dad stalked out, jaw set, eyes blazing. Taylor imagined steam blasting from his ears, and pulled his feet in close to avoid getting stepped on.

Luke followed, frowning as he grabbed his suitcase, sleeping bag and pillow, and hurried to catch up with his dad. His suitcase ran over Marissa's toe.

"Ow!" She grabbed her foot. "You jerk!"

Luke didn't stop to apologize. "Dad, wait up."

His dad's voice came back loud and clear, though he must have been outside. "Do not tell me what to do. Do not speak until I say you can talk. Not another word out of you until then. Understand? Not. One."

A grin crept across Taylor's face. "I bet he doesn't get that Corvette he was planning on." Weird. He actually felt a little sorry for Luke. Dad's wrath would come soon enough, and Taylor wouldn't wish that on anyone.

Marissa grimaced and rubbed her toe. "I bet he did that on purpose."

Taylor shushed her, but the door to Zeke's office closed again. What more did Zeke and Roberto have to say to Dad? He leaned his ear closer to the door.

"Can you hear them?" Marissa whispered.

Taylor shook his head. Dad wouldn't explode in front of Zeke. Maybe he'd have chilled a bit by the time they drove home. Or maybe that was too much to hope for.

Ten minutes later, the door opened. Taylor scrambled to his feet while Dad shook hands with Zeke and said good-bye. The director came out and put his arm around Taylor. "Will we see you back next year?"

"I hope so." Taylor shot a glance at Dad as he exited the office behind Roberto. Despite the grim expression, Taylor saw none of the controlled fury that he expected.

Zeke put a hand on Marissa's shoulder. "You remember what we talked about. I look forward to seeing how you've grown next year."

Marissa nodded, snuck a peek at Dad and glanced uneasily at Taylor.

Taylor responded with his own uncertain gaze. Even Dad's voice sounded firm but calm.

"Take your sister's suitcase and let's go. You kids can load up while I take a look at this car."

Taylor took hold of Marissa's suitcase and dragged it toward the door. He'd have liked to keep up with Dad and Roberto, to listen in as they talked about cars, but when they reached the parking lot, he and Marissa veered off to stow their luggage in the van.

Marissa threw her sleeping bag into the back. "I don't get why guys are so fascinated with cars. I mean, I know some look cooler than others, but they're all just chunks of metal." She opened the flap of her purse and dug around inside.

Taylor grunted as he lifted her suitcase into the van. "Yeah, the same way purses are all hunks of fabric. So what's the big deal? Why's one worth hundreds of dollars just because someone's name is on it?"

"Okay, but at least we don't discuss purses for hours and hours." She pulled her cell phone out of her purse. "I'll be right back."

"Where you going?" Taylor called after her as she dashed toward the machine shed.

19
———

Taylor hesitated before following at a slower pace. Seeing the Mustang all messed up left a lump in the pit of his stomach. Maybe next year, Roberto would have it ready to drive and they could go for a ride in it. Dad and Roberto were inside, still talking engine sizes and mechanics, so Taylor stopped outside. Dad was going to be really ticked off at him for working on the car after being told to stay away from them.

Marissa approached the two men and waited in silence until they paused to look her way. "Is it okay if I take some pictures of your car?"

Roberto nodded. "Si! Is okay."

Frowning, Dad continued his conversation with Roberto about the cost of the repairs, how much Roberto would do himself, and the process of restoring a vintage car. His eyes followed Marissa as she took pictures of the mangled front end from different angles, plus some close-ups of the broken headlights, the crumpled bumper and the scratched hood.

Finally, Dad shook Roberto's hand and called to Marissa, his voice firm but not harsh. "That's enough, Marissa. What are you going to do with all those pictures?"

Marissa held her phone to her chest. "I'm keeping them right here to remind me."

Storm clouds gathered on Dad's face. "To remind you? Shame on you—"

"Daddy! Let me finish. It's to remind me to think about my decisions before I ruin my life or someone else's." She turned to Roberto. "I know I said it before with Zeke, but I really am sorry about the car, Mr. Rodriguez."

Roberto smiled at her. "Is good to learn from mistakes. I forgive you." He turned to Taylor. "You come back next year. We take ride in car." He shook Taylor's hand, holding it firm. His kind eyes brought a lump to Taylor's throat.

He choked out the words. "I'll be back. Thanks for letting me help you."

Dad still stared at Marissa. He swallowed hard before rasping out, "Time to go." He nodded to Roberto and motioned to Marissa and Taylor, but said nothing more as they got into the van.

Taylor skipped his usual argument with Marissa for shotgun position and climbed into one of the captain's chairs in the second row. Marissa claimed the other one. She must be as wary as he was about sitting up front with Dad. Taylor pulled out his magazine and settled in for the ride home.

Several minutes down the road, Marissa tapped Taylor's arm and tipped her head toward Dad, her eyebrows drawing together in a question.

Taylor shrugged. *How should I know?* Dad had never given them the silent treatment before. It was odd that he wasn't saying anything. Nothing at all. But no doubt, he'd let them have it when he was ready to talk.

Ten minutes later, Taylor had dozed off. He startled when Marissa kicked his foot. Sitting up, he scowled at her, but she pointed at Dad's back and mouthed the words, *Say something.* Taylor shook his head, settled back in the seat, and turned his attention once more to his car magazine. He'd need to look for a new one when he got home. This one was getting old.

Half an hour later, Marissa broke the silence. "Daddy?" She used her little girl voice, the one that always worked on Dad. "Aren't you going to say anything?"

Dad glanced at them in the rearview mirror. "I'm thinking, Marissa. We'll talk later, not right now."

Eyes wide and brimming, Marissa shrank back into the seat. She plugged her ears with earbuds, and scrolled through her phone for some music. A tear splashed onto her hand and she wiped it against her shorts.

Taylor stretched his legs and snuggled his head back against the headrest. Whatever was going to happen apparently wouldn't happen until they got home. He closed his eyes and the next time he opened them, they were pulling into their driveway at home.

Dad brought the car to a stop, telling Taylor to stay put as he shut it off. "Marissa, you go on in the house. I need to talk with your brother. We'll bring the stuff in when we're done."

Uh-oh. Taylor sat up and rubbed his face, trying to wake up. His neck was sore from sleeping at a weird angle, and he wiped spit from his chin where he must have been drooling.

"But Daddy, it wasn't Taylor's fault."

Dad cut her off. "Go inside, please, Marissa."

She pressed her lips together and glanced at Taylor, a scared look in her eyes as she slid the van's side door closed and walked toward the house.

Here it comes.

Dad turned around in his seat. "Pastor Zacharias and Mr. Rodriguez both had very complimentary things to say about you."

Taylor waited.

Dad looked down at the floor. "Luke's dad agreed to pay 75% of the cost of repairs if I pay 25%. I don't like it, but I agreed. Marissa was involved, even though she wasn't wholly responsible." He paused, his jaw working back and forth. His foot scraped at a stain on the carpet. "I've been thinking about ordering one of those do-it-yourself driver training courses, to help with your driver's ed class."

Taylor cut off the beginning of a chuckle. "You mean, I get to take driver's ed?"

"We'll sign you up next week. But I'd like to have a hand in teaching you. It'll give us something to do together." Dad rubbed the bristly five o'clock shadow on his cheek. "It seems other people know my son better than I do. Kind of embarrassing, y'know what I mean?" A rare smile touched Dad's lips, though sadness shaded his eyes.

Taylor had never seen that before, but his breath escaped him as he realized he was going to get his driver's license. His lips refused to stay in a straight line, spreading out in a wide grin. "Thanks, Dad."

Dad swung around and opened the door. "Let's get the stuff and get into the house before Mom wonders what happened to us."

Taylor hopped out of the car. The way his heart soared, he could probably fly all the way back to Rustic Knoll. This time next year, he'd have his driver's license and maybe— just maybe, Roberto would let him drive the Mustang around camp. Man, he couldn't wait!

If you've enjoyed this novel, please consider leaving the author a review. Your thoughts and feedback are very much appreciated.

DISCUSSION QUESTIONS

1. What dreams or goals do you have that seem unattainable? What keeps you from striving to reach them? Have you shared them with someone who will dream with you?

2. "Being stuck between a princess and a prince stinks." What made Taylor feel this way? Have you ever been jealous of the way your siblings are treated compared to you? How did you handle it?

3. Much of Greek and Roman mythology attempts to explain certain aspects of life on earth. What event or problem does the myth of Pandora's bottle try to explain? How does the Bible explain this same event?

4. Luke 6:45 says whatever is in our heart will make itself known by what comes out of our mouth. What does your speech reveal about what's in your heart?

5. Claire didn't use foul language even when Taylor made her fall headlong into the mud. Why did this impress Taylor? Do you know any kids who refrain from cursing and using obscene language? How do

you feel about that? How do you think they manage to
keep their speech pure, to "speak no evil"?

6. How do the words Roberto speaks to Taylor differ
   from the words Taylor's dad speaks? Which would you
   rather hear? Do your words more closely resemble
   Roberto's or Dad's?

7. Taylor is known for his verbal bullying. How does he
   react when Luke bullies him?

8. If actions speak louder than words, what is Taylor
   saying by his actions toward Luke? Toward Marissa?

9. Zeke discussed problems of foul language, anger and
   jealousy, pride and arrogance, lying and deceitfulness.
   How does each play a part in Taylor's week at camp?

10. Taylor discovers that jealousy and anger toward his
    brother, his sister, Brady and Luke is the root
    motivation for his bullying. How might the other heart
    issues listed in Question 8 motivate someone to bully
    others?

11. What are the parallels between restoring the Mustang
    and what happens to our heart when we put our faith
    and trust in Jesus? What are some differences?

12. Taylor was willing to sacrifice himself and his dreams
    for the things he cared about. How does this illustrate
    Jesus' love for us?

RESOURCES

Abuse: If you or someone you know is hurt by verbal or physical abuse, it's important to talk to someone you trust. This could be a pastor, school counselor, a trusted teacher, a friend's parent, or a neighbor. Abuse is NOT your fault, so don't be embarrassed about it.

Bullying is unwanted, aggressive behavior among school-aged children that includes actions such as making threats, spreading rumors, and attacking someone verbally or physically. Learn more at StopBullying.gov

Christian Camps: To find one in your area, type "Christian Youth Camps" and your state into any search engine. Or go to the Christian Camp and Conference Association: www.ccca.org

ACKNOWLEDGMENTS

I am indebted to Rich Bullock, who answered this automotively-challenged writer's call for help and patiently explained the steps of restoring a classic Mustang. And he did so in terms I actually understood.

Special thanks to Paul Siegmann for reminding me of the God Squad, and to Donna Watson. You both provided valuable feedback on the finished manuscript for which I am very grateful.

Deb Garland, Peggy Wirgau, Terri Wangard, and Tanya Eavenson are not only precious friends, but the best critique partners ever. Words can't express my appreciation for your friendship and your willingness to give an honest evaluation, many times on a moment's notice. I've learned so much from your comments and suggestions.

Family and friends provided constant encouragement and support, making the long process of writing a little easier. Thanks to my encouraging husband, Wayne, who acts as a sounding board for ideas. And to my three incredible kids, Daniel, Beki, and Matt who willingly answer the occasional odd question about teenage vocabulary or how a teen would react in a certain situation. I'm also deeply grateful for the members of my Grace

Awakening class and other friends who consistently provide encouragement for my writing journey.

Finally, my deepest and humblest gratitude goes to my God and Savior, without whom I'd have no basis at all for this story. He is willing and able to restore that which is lost, broken, and discarded. We are each precious and valuable in his sight.

ABOUT THE AUTHOR

Mary L. Hamilton grew up at a camp in southern Wisconsin much like the setting for her Rustic Knoll novels. Her experiences during twenty years of living at the camp, as well as people she knew there, inspired many of the events and situations in her novels.

When not writing, Mary enjoys reading, knitting, being outdoors and spending time with her family. She and her husband make their home in Texas.

Connect with Mary:
www.MaryHamiltonBooks.com
www.Facebook.com/MaryHamiltonBooks
www.Pinterest.com/mhamiltonbooks

More Books in the
Rustic Knoll Bible Camp Series
Hear No Evil, Book 1
Brady McCaul struggles to understand his mother's sudden rejection when she drops him off at camp, only to discover it was for his own protection.

See No Evil, Book 3
Steven Miller guards a dark secret. Can he prevent his friend from pursuing a similar course without exposing his own shameful past?

Sneak Peak

See No Evil
Rustic Knoll Bible Camp Series Book 3

CHAPTER 1

Steven Miller pulled away from his mom's hand as she straightened his t-shirt before getting out of the car. "It's fine, Mom. Leave it alone."

Blindness was no excuse for sloppy dressing, but this was camp. Some guys wore the same clothes they'd slept in the night before. He got out of the car, leaving behind its air-conditioned comfort. Ugh! This heat wave would make the cabins feel like saunas. He adjusted his dark glasses, then reached into the back seat and found the rough canvas of his duffle bag.

"Can I get that for you?" Mom's door slammed and her footsteps hurried around to his side.

"I've got it." *As if I'm not capable of doing it myself.* He bit his tongue as he lifted the bag out of the car and set it on the gravel parking lot. Mom wasn't trying to be annoying. So why did she get on his nerves so easily lately? She'd always watched out for him during Dad's tough lessons on living with blindness. 'Survival for the Blind 101,' they'd called it. Had she grown more protective in the three years since Dad died? Or maybe Dad's absence failed to balance out Mom's hovering. Either way, it would be nice if she'd back off a little.

Claire called from somewhere nearby. "Steven! Wait for me!"

Where is she? Car engines and voices of other excited campers made it hard to tell which direction she was calling from. He waved his hand in the air to acknowledge her, then closed the car door and leaned against it. "Mom, you don't have to stick around. Claire can get me through registration."

Mom stuttered. "Well, II'm not in any hurry."

He'd done it again—said something the wrong way. "I'm not trying to get rid of you. I just thought Claire could get me up to the check-in table and I'm sure I can make it to the cabin on my own if you want to get home earlier."

At that moment, Claire arrived and gave him a quick hug around the neck. "Great to see you again, Steven. Ooh! You've been working out. Look at those muscles." She squeezed his upper arm. "Hi, Mrs. Miller. Can you believe it's our last year at Rustic Knoll? This time next year, we'll be graduated and getting ready for college."

Mrs. Miller groaned. "Don't remind me. Seems like last week you two were playing in the sand together down at the lake. With your blonde hair and Steven's, everyone thought you were twins."

Claire laughed. "That was a long time ago." She touched Steven's arm. "Are you ready to go check in?"

Mom made no move to leave. "Are your parents here, Claire?"

"No. My younger brother has a Little League tournament today, so Mom dropped me off. She'll have to hurry to make the game. But I can take Steven to check-in if you want. Dillon's heading our way, too. He can make sure Steven gets to his cabin."

Mom hesitated. "Are you sure?"

Steven reached out and Mom put her hand in his. "We'll be fine, Mom. We know the routine. You really don't need to stick around, unless you want to see some of the other parents."

She sighed, hugged his neck and kissed his cheek. He jerked away before she could swipe her fingers over his hair.

"You have your health form? And money for snacks?"

"I have everything I need. Honest, I'll be fine, Mom. I'll send you a postcard like always. Saturday will be here before you know it."

"All right, then. Have a good week, both of you. I love you, Steven." She hugged him one more time.

"Love you, too, Mom. Bye!"

The car door squeaked open and closed, and a moment later, the engine started. She called one more good-bye before the tires crunched on the gravel as she drove away. Steven let out a long breath. "Good thing you came by. I was afraid she might walk me to the cabin and stay to tuck me into bed tonight."

Claire giggled. "I love your mom, but I feel the same way about mine. I can't wait to get out of the house and be on my own."

Dillon shuffled up, dragging his suitcase. "Hey, Claire! Steven-man, how's it going?" His hand met Steven's in a high five and they clamped their hands tight together. "Ow! Dude, you must be lifting weights. Look at those biceps."

Steven grinned. "I'm giving you some competition for super-jock this year. You ready?"

Dillon chuckled. "I'm always ready for competition."

"Come on, let's check in." Claire nudged Steven's arm. "You want to hold on?"

"No thanks. I'm practicing my echolocation."

"Your what?" Claire started toward the grass where the registration table sat.

"Echolocation." Dillon snorted. "Isn't that what bats use?"

"Euw!"

"Same idea." Steven walked close beside Claire. "It's figuring out the sounds around me to judge my location. Like right now, I'm judging my distance from you by the sound of your feet hitting the ground." Claire's steps moved farther away, and Steven adjusted his own path to follow her.

"Okay. Just testing," Claire said. "You passed."

"It's easy here, but grass tends to muffle sound." Just then, they moved onto the grass, but Claire's flip-flops made it easy to follow them. They had to be getting close to the registration table. A warm breeze rustled the leaves of the trees overhead and carried a whiff of the lake that lay beyond the dining hall. Steven inhaled the familiar scent as Claire brought them to a stop. He set his duffle beside him. "How long is the line? Do you see anyone else we know?"

Claire moved forward a couple steps. "Taylor and Marissa are up ahead."

Dillon grunted at Taylor's name. "I wouldn't admit to knowing him."

"He's not as bad as he used to be." Claire tugged Steven forward. "Give him a chance. He's changed."

Dillon scoffed. "Hey! Who's the new lady? Where's Nurse Willie?"

"What?" Steven's hand moved to his chest. "What are you talking about?"

Claire braced herself on Steven's shoulder and jumped for a better view. "Some Asian lady's checking people in. I don't see Nurse Willie anywhere."

Dillon pulled his suitcase closer as the line moved forward. "Wonder what happened to ol' Willie."

"Maybe she had something to do today." Claire made it sound more like a question.

"If she's busy, why not use one of the counselors?" Steven scratched his ear.

"Maybe she left, got a job somewhere else," Dillon suggested.

Nurse Willie leave Rustic Knoll? *Impossible.* She hadn't missed an opening day of camp in all the years he'd been coming to Rustic Knoll. Ever since he was five years old and asked his dad about the tinkling sound her hat made, she'd always been there to take his health form, wearing her bucket hat decorated with fishing lures. Steven's fingers traced the edges of the medallion hidden beneath his shirt. It stuck to his skin in the afternoon heat.

Before long, an unfamiliar voice called, "Next!"

Claire moved ahead to the registration table, urging Steven along with her. A crinkling of paper reminded him to pull out his health form.

"Welcome to Rustic Knoll," the new voice said. "You areClaire Thompson?" The woman spoke with an accent, pronouncing her words as precisely as the Vietnamese lady who lived down the street from Steven.

"Yes, ma'am," Claire answered. "Where's Nurse Willie?"

"She's had some health problems. I'm Mrs. Hoang. I'm taking her place until she gets better."

"Mrs. Wang?"

"No. H-wang." Steven corrected Claire by exhaling on the first letter.

"Very good!" Mrs. Hoang said.

"How did you know that?" Claire asked.

Steven pointed to his ears. "Being blind means I have to listen harder." He held out his health form toward Mrs. Hoang. "Steven Miller. Is Nurse Willie all right?" Dillon moved up next to him.

"Pastor Zacharias will make an announcement at supper."

"But is she okay?" Claire asked.

Several seconds passed. Was she checking his health form?

"You'll have to ask Pastor Zacharias," Mrs. Hoang sighed. "I don't want to say too much."

Claire's fingers clamped around Steven's arm as they received cabin assignments and moved away from the table. They stopped to wait for Dillon. Her breath carried a minty scent when she spoke in his ear. "It can't be good when she won't give us a straight answer."

Steven searched for an explanation. "Maybe it's something personal and she doesn't want it blurted out in front of everyone."

Dillon joined them. "Pastor Zacharias? Who calls him that?"

Claire mimicked Mrs. Hoang. "I'm going to find 'Pastor Zacharias' and ask what's up with Willie. You guys want to come along?"

Steven waited for Dillon's response, but it never came. He lifted his arm that carried the sleeping bag and pillow. "Can we unload our stuff in the cabin first?"

"I suppose. Meet you in fifteen minutes."

"What's the rush?" Dillon grumbled.

Claire's sigh screamed impatience. "Just get back here as soon as you can or I won't bother to wait for you." She headed off toward her cabin.

Dillon nudged Steven toward the guys' cabins. "It's not like she's dying or something. That Wang lady said she's here until Willie gets better."

"H-wang."

"That's what I said. Wang. So, how long have you been lifting weights?"

Steven shook his head, pulled his suitcase around and kept pace with the flapping of Dillon's sandals. "I started last winter when I decided to do a triathlon."

"You're doing a triathlon? A real one?"

"Not a long one like the Ironman. Sprint triathlons are half the Olympic distances, so I swim a quarter mile, bike about twelve miles, and run a little over three miles. They're held all over the Chicago area through October, but the one I'm doing is at the end of August, about five weeks from now." Grass tickled the sides of his feet, and the perfume of roses told him they were passing the garden beside the chapel.

"So you're competing along with sighted people? Wouldn't that be dangerous with the size crowds they attract?"

"I'd be tethered to a partner for swimming and running, and use a tandem for the bicycle part of it."

"They let you do that?"

"I've applied for permission from the race officials. Hoping I'll hear this week." Steven hefted his sleeping bag higher on his hip.

"Who's your partner?"

"As of last Tuesday, I don't know. The guy I've been training with is having knee problems. You want to fill in for him?"

Dillon hopped up the cabin steps. "Maybe. Sounds cool."

The screen door squawked when Dillon opened it. Every cabin's screen door sounded like that. Steven had been in all four of the Rustic Knoll boys' cabins over the years. They all had the same floor plan, the same furniture in the common room. He entered the cabin and strode past the couch and easy chairs in their assigned places, stopping at the doorway to the bunkroom.

Dillon spoke over Steven's shoulder. "The bunk to your right is open. I'll take the top if you promise no earthquakes."

Steven laughed. "It's tempting, but I think I'm past that prank."

Every kid who'd ever come to camp had lain on a bottom bunk, braced his feet against the top bunk and pushed up while yelling "Earthquake!" Steven had been the unsuspecting top bunk occupant once and nearly got pitched off onto the concrete floor. He'd claimed the bottom bunk ever since, and now spread his sleeping bag out on the mattress, stowing his suitcase below the bed.

Dylan followed, throwing his stuff onto the bunk above Steven's and zipping open his suitcase. "What got you interested in triathlons?"

Steven straightened. He fingered the cord around his neck, hesitating to share something so treasured. Finally, he drew the large medallion out from under his shirt and held it in his palm for Dillon to see.

"This was my dad's. Mom found it when she was cleaning out some of his stuff this past year. I didn't know he did triathlons, but she said he'd done a couple before I was born."

Sweaty fingers grazed Steven's as Dillon turned the medallion over and back. "That's cool. Bet it's nice having something of your dad's, huh?"

"Yeah, it's a nice reminder." Steven cupped it in his hand before dropping it down inside his shirt again. Not that he needed anything to remind him Dad had once been alive and well, a triathlon finisher. *If it wasn't for me, Dad might still be alive.*

The screen door screeched and Brady entered the bunkroom. "There you are. I've been checking every cabin looking for you." He high-fived Steven, exchanged greetings with Dillon, then plopped down on Steven's bed. "Do you know what happened to Nurse Willie? Why wasn't she at check-in?"

Dillon flipped the lid on his suitcase closed and pushed it under Steven's bed. "She's sick. That's what Mrs. Hoang said."

"Who's that? Oh, the other lady? How do you say her name?"

"H-wang." Steven squeezed past Dillon. "We're meeting Claire to go ask Zeke what's up. You want to come, too?"

"Sure."

The three of them exited the cabin and met Claire near the Snack Shack. She greeted Brady, then led the way to Zeke's office. "I don't have a good feeling about this."

A weight settled in Steven's stomach as well, but he'd wait to hear what Zeke said. The four friends crowded through the open door of the camp director's office.

"Looks like the gang's all here." Zeke chuckled. "What can I do for you?"

Steven moved far enough into the room to rest his hand on the smooth wooden desktop. A faint musty smell of paper drew his attention. Over the years, he'd imagined Zeke's office lined with shelves crammed full of books. Is that where he kept his Bible, the one Brady said he carried to chapel? At some time during his years at Rustic Knoll, Steven had learned the outer walls of Zeke's office held two large windows that he kept open to catch the breeze off the lake. No breeze today, but Steven still caught a whiff of sand and water.

"What's wrong with Nurse Willie?" Claire always did come right to the point.

A soft sigh came from Zeke's lips. "Late last summer, she complained of headaches. She went in for some tests and they found a brain tumor. Surgery removed most of it, but it's something she'll have to live with."

"Cancer?" Steven's stomach turned to a rock. "A brain tumor?"

"What causes that?" Claire's voice almost cracked.

"They don't really know what causes brain tumors."

"How bad is she?" Steven swallowed bile. Did he really want to hear the answer?

"It will probably grow again, but for now, the chemo seems to have put it into remission."

Brady sank onto one of the armchairs in front of Zeke's desk. "She's not well enough to work?"

"The doctor says she should be, but she's not bouncing back the way we expected. I think she's experiencing some depression, which is not unusual." Zeke's glasses tapped against the desk. "We're the only family she has, so she's still in her apartment at the back of the clinic. Mrs. Hoang agreed to stay in the guesthouse. Willie helps Mrs. Hoang whenever she's able, but I think seeing someone else in her clinic hasn't helped her attitude."

Steven leaned against the desk. "Can we visit her?"

"Not all of you at once. Talk to Mrs. Hoang. She'll know when Willie is up for having visitors."

Claire expelled a heavy breath. "It's not the same without Nurse Willie."

Zeke shuffled some papers. "I'm sure seeing you kids will cheer her up. She needs your prayers, and Mrs. Hoang could use a few, too. It's been hard on everyone and filling Nurse Willie's shoes has been especially difficult."

Steven turned to leave the office, and the others followed him in silence. No slapping of flip-flops now. Their feet shuffled, as sluggish as an August breeze.

A brain tumor. Willie didn't deserve this, not after all her years of digging splinters out of fingers, dispensing bandages, checking for fevers, wrapping sprained ankles and broken bones, hunting down kids who forgot to come and take their medicine at the proper time. She'd taken good care of him that time he and Brady got into poison ivy.

As soon as they were outside, Claire spoke up. "I'm going down to see her. Who wants to come with me?"

Steven didn't answer. Zeke said seeing all of them would cheer Willie up, but did he really want to visit her? Wasn't there something else he could do to help, something more than visiting her?

Finally, Dillon spoke up. "Sorry. I'm going swimming. Anyone else going back to the cabin?"

Brady volunteered. "Yeah, I'll go back with you," Brady said.

"Steven?"

The pleading in Claire's voice almost got him. "I'll go later, but tell her I said hi."

He shouldn't leave Claire to visit by herself, but he wasn't ready for Nurse Willie yet. Unwanted memories and doubts of Dad's death rushed back. Still, he couldn't sit by and do nothing when someone he cared about was sick, maybe dying. He never wanted to do that again.

Ever.

Made in United States
Orlando, FL
12 April 2023

32024993R00114